# Like Cats & Dogs

Based on the Hallmark Channel Original Movie

Alexis Stanton

Like Cats and Dogs



ISBN: 978-1-947892-17-0

Hallmark PUBLISHING

www.hallmarkpublishing.com

For more about the movie visit:
http://www.hallmarkchannel.com/like-cats-dogs

# Table of Contents

# Chapter One

Just as the train pulled into the South Haven station, Laura Haley's phone buzzed. Laura rarely travelled by train, and she'd spent the journey from Lansing feeling like an elegant heroine in one of the classic movies she loved so much. She suppressed a sigh when she saw that the caller was her mother. So much for feeling glamorous.

*Do I answer it?* Laura wondered as she rose from her seat to get her luggage. She wasn't even a minute into her vacation, and already they were checking on her.

As if sensing her distress, Laura's dog Frank whined and tugged on his leash. She gave the part-beagle, part-who-knew-what a comforting rub on his head before finally picking up.

"Hey, Mom." Laura tried to hide her impatience. But for goodness' sake, she was twenty-three, not ten. A college graduate, even. She didn't need her parents monitoring her every movement.

Passengers began collecting their bags and heading toward the exit. Laura took her duffle bag and rolling suitcase from the luggage rack—no easy feat considering she also juggled Frank's leash and her cell phone. Her mismatched bags didn't help, either, with their varying sizes and weights. She was good at filing multiple tax returns, but much less organized when it came to just about everything else.

"Honey?" Her mother's concerned voice came through clearly despite the hum of activity surrounding Laura. "Where are you? Did you make your train? Have you arrived?"

As if her mother could see her, Laura pasted on a smile while she stepped onto the platform. "Yes, Mom, I'm getting off the train right now."

"We were worried when we didn't hear from you."

Movement surrounded Laura on all sides. People hurried with their bags, and passengers were being greeted by relatives and, *oh, brother*, significant others.

*I'm here alone by choice*, she reminded herself. *Besides, I'm not alone. I have Frank.*

The dog strained on his leash, excited by all the commotion, and she struggled to keep hold of him while also talking to her mother and muscling her bags down the platform.

"I told you," Laura said with enforced patience, "I would call as soon as I got to the rental place." She stopped to adjust a strap on her suitcase.

"We're already at wits' end here."

"Mom, it's only for two weeks. I'm sure you and Dad will be fine." She glanced around at the other passengers hustling back and forth. Was it her imagination, or were they sending her pitying glances?

*One year out of college and I'm still my parents' little girl.*

"I don't know," her mother said, and Laura could practically hear her pacing up and down in the kitchen of the family home. "It's April. It gets so hectic here in April."

Laura grabbed hold of her suitcase handle and trudged with it into the station, all the while praying Frank wouldn't tug her arm right out of its socket with his eagerness.

"Yes, I know it's our busy season, Mom," she said briskly. "You were the ones who also told me I needed a vacation, so, here I am."

Tax season was always a frenzy at Haley & Haley Accounting, but Laura had made certain that she'd taken care of all her clients' filings before going on vacation. She'd never leave her parents in the lurch—

especially since they not only employed her but housed her as well.

All of her friends from college lived on their own, and none of them worked for their parents. Not her. Without a clear plan after graduation, she'd moved back home and reluctantly gone to Haley & Haley for the same job she'd had every summer since sophomore year of high school.

*What's wrong with me? Why can't I figure out what I want?*

Hopefully, this time away in South Haven, Michigan, would help clear her head a little. At the least, she'd get some much-needed time away from her parents—and memories of yet another failed relationship.

Her mother said, "Don't forget to hold on to all your paperwork."

Frank whined louder and tugged hard on the leash. Something had gotten his attention.

"I will keep my receipts. Don't worry." Laura tried to hold tighter to Frank, but he wriggled with the need to run.

"Of course you will," her mother said with satisfaction. "You're the daughter of two accountants." She exhaled. "I hope you have a good time, honey. We love you."

"I love you, too." They might be a touch

overprotective, and a little straitlaced, but there was no denying the fact that her parents cared about their only child and just wanted the best for her.

She'd barely pressed the button to end the call when Frank gave one last tug on the leash. He broke free, and her stomach dropped as he went tearing through the station, weaving between passengers. Clearly, he pursued something that had caught his attention.

Laura sprinted after him. "Frank! Frank!"

Just like his master, her dog refused to be sensible. He barked with excitement as he ran, causing people to stop and stare.

Laura didn't have time to be embarrassed. She had to grab her dog before he ran right out of the station and hurried off to get lost in the lakeside town. "*Frank*!"

Her dog came to an abrupt stop in front of a hard-sided animal carrier perched on a rolling luggage cart. He continued to bark while he pawed at the plastic. Inside the carrier, a long-haired cat the color of smoke hissed in response to its harassment.

A blond man crouched in front of the carrier, as though protecting the cat. "Whoa, down, boy," he said to Frank. "Down."

Grabbing hold of the leash, Laura pulled Frank back. "He got away from me. I'm sorry."

The man looked up at her, and all she could see

for a moment were striking blue eyes, bright with intelligence. Trying to collect herself, she saw that the rest of the man was just as striking. He had the face of a fairy-tale prince, with full lips and square jaw. His fair hair was neatly combed. In fact, everything about him was neat, from the collar of his shirt peeking out above the neckline of his sweater to his navy blazer and pressed khakis.

*Cute, but not my type,* she told herself. Yet she stared at him anyway.

Maybe she was imagining things, but he stared right back at her as if snared in some kind of spell.

Finally, he blinked, collecting himself. "Uh…that's okay." He straightened but said to the cat, "You all right, Mozart?"

Interesting name for a cat, considering the origins of Frank's name. "Mozart?"

"Yes," the handsome stranger said. "After the composer."

She quirked an eyebrow at him. "I know who Mozart is."

He gave her a small, sheepish smile. "I'm sure you do. No offense." He bent down to look at his cat. "You okay, Mozart? Is this mean dog scaring you?"

"Frank's not really mean."

"Frank," the stranger repeated.

"After the singer," she said, her words dry.

He ducked his head a little, acknowledging his own faux pas. Still, his gaze remained locked with hers. A moment passed before he said with an attempt at politeness, "Well. Anyway. Excuse me. Hope you have a nice day."

"You, too." She felt oddly disappointed as the cat owner pushed the cart away, taking his pet and matched luggage with him as he made his way to the exit.

*That was interesting.*

And fleeting. She was alone with Frank in the bustling station.

"You're not really mean, are you, Frank?" she asked the dog. In response, he wagged his tail. It never failed to make her smile. "No, you're not. Let's go."

She went back and, with Frank's leash clasped firmly in her hand, collected her luggage. Good thing South Haven was a small town, because her bags were right where she'd left them. If anyone had stolen her stuff—especially the bag with her camera—she would've been devastated.

But everything was fine, and, after gathering up the luggage, she took a deep breath and made for the exit. Her vacation started right now. There would be nothing but relaxation for the next two weeks.

*It really shouldn't be this difficult,* Spencer Hodkins thought as he stood in front of the car rental counter.

But perhaps he was being too demanding. He was still thinking about the adorable blonde with the dog—Frank, for Frank Sinatra, which charmed him—and probably wasn't articulating his specific needs to the rental agent very well.

He glanced behind him at the line. Nobody looked very happy that he was taking so long, but he liked what he liked, and if he was going to have the expense of a rental car, it needed to meet his needs.

"It should have wireless capabilities," he said to the agent, who looked back at him with her best customer service face. "Electric, obviously." He wanted to be as eco-conscious as possible. "And, if it has a sunroof, it should have a UV coating on the interior glass as well."

When his cell chirped, he said to the agent, "Excuse me for a second." He turned away slightly to answer the call—it was Susan. "Hi, honey," he said when the pretty brunette's face appeared on the screen. She was, as usual, perfectly groomed, her hair neatly contained by a headband and a string of elegant pearls encircling her neck.

For some reason, he thought again of the girl from the station, and her tousled blond locks. She'd looked like some wild elf who'd just emerged from the forest.

Whoever she was, she'd seemed the exact opposite of Susan, in every way.

"Just getting my rental car," he said to Susan.

"Electric?" she asked.

"Obviously."

"UV? You know how you burn."

He smiled at that. Susan always tried to take care of him. "I'm not going to be outside that much, anyway. I have two weeks to finish my dissertation." He shoved down the panic that rose up whenever he thought of his lengthy paper and everything it represented.

"Well, I'm glad to hear that," Susan said crisply. "You really need to focus, Spencer. My father doesn't give out grants to just anybody."

"I know." Dr. Philip Drake wasn't only Susan's father; he was also the head of the university's psychology department. Spencer's whole future rested on Dr. Drake's approval. The thought made Spencer's stomach clench in anxiety, but he took a breath, forcing himself to be calm. Emotions were merely chemical reactions, and he could control that.

The people behind him in line grumbled at the holdup.

"Hey," he said to Susan, "I've got to go."

"Call me later," she answered in a tone that commanded him to do exactly that.

"I will." Automatically, he added, "I love—"

Susan ended the call.

"You." He ignored the stab of disappointment that went through him. Susan was Susan. She liked everything on her terms. Just like Spencer wanted everything to be precise and orderly. They were perfect for each other. No messy feelings, no unruly emotions. Yes, perfect.

"My girlfriend," he said by way of explanation to the people behind him. "She worries."

No one said anything back, but a few of them scowled.

With an apologetic shrug, he turned back to the waiting agent. He needed to get to the rental house as soon as possible and start working. The world of research was just as controlled and safe as his relationship with Susan—exactly how he wanted it.

# Chapter Two

*I think I'm in love.*

Enamored, Laura watched South Haven pass by her as she and Frank rode in a cab toward the rental house. Everywhere she looked, she found something else she loved about the small town.

Mature trees were everywhere, so different from the antiseptic Lansing suburb where she lived. Adorable independent businesses lined the main street, unlike the chain stores that dominated the malls of her hometown. Here and there she saw banners announcing an upcoming spring art fair, which, as luck would have it, coincided with her stay in South Haven. The homes were a charming mix of vintage brick and wood houses and sleek modern structures. It was precisely the sort of place she needed in her life.

The cab drove along the shoreline, passing a wooden pier, and she watched with fascination as the late-afternoon sunlight gleamed on the water.

If the water's bright hue reminded her of the cat owner's blue eyes, she would just chalk it up to watching too many old movies starring a young, idealistic Henry Fonda.

Frank planted his front feet on the window, just as entranced by the town as his owner.

She pulled her cell from her pocket and dialed. Within a few rings, a familiar voice answered.

"Laura?" Rose Chang exclaimed.

"I'm here! Heading toward my rental." She glanced out the window. "This place is so beautiful. No wonder you love living here."

"I can't wait to see you," Rose gushed. "How long has it been?"

"Since your wedding, right?" Laura shook her head in disbelief. Where had the time gone? She'd been sleepwalking her way through life since graduation.

"A whole year?" Rose asked in disbelief. "That's crazy. We've got a lot of catching up to do."

Laura almost bounced with eagerness. She and Rose had been through all of college's craziness together, and maybe when they saw each other, they might be able to rekindle some of that fire and excitement her current existence lacked.

"Just let me get settled in at the house," she said, "and we'll go out. First margarita's on me."

There was a tiny pause. "Uh...about that," Rose said.

"What?" Laura laughed. "Come on. Don't tell me you've changed that much since college."

"Like I said," Rose said slowly, "we've got a lot of catching up to do. I'll see you later."

Laura frowned in puzzlement. It wasn't like Rose to be evasive. She'd been so outspoken when they'd been in school, always the first onstage at the karaoke bar, dragging Laura up with her. They'd belted out "Que Sera, Sera" and "Diamonds Are a Girl's Best Friend" more times than Laura could count.

"Okay," she finally said. "I'll see you later."

She ended the call and sat in pensive silence for the rest of the taxi ride while stroking Frank's sleek fur. Yet again, she had the feeling that everyone she'd known was moving forward, making progress, while she continued to sleep in her childhood bedroom, surrounded by tacked-up movie posters, and spinning her wheels.

But she wasn't here in South Haven to brood. She was here to get inspiration, relax, and spend time with Rose. Even though Rose was married to Kenny now—a really terrific guy—it could be like old times again, when the future didn't matter.

She asked the cab driver to stop briefly at the local market, where she bought a few groceries, including a nice bottle of white wine. It was a financial indulgence, but what the heck. She was on vacation.

Her mood lightened further when the cab pulled up outside the most gorgeous house she'd ever seen. It was a modern home of stone, fronting the lake, with a wide curving driveway leading up to its sizeable front doors. The best part about the two-story structure was that it was all hers. She could turn her music up and sing along without her father grousing about the volume. She could take long, luxurious showers, using tons of towels, and wouldn't have to face her mother's baleful looks of reproach.

"Wow…" she said as the taxi driver got out to grab her bags.

She opened the cab's door and stepped out, careful to keep a grip on Frank's leash. Once she'd paid and tipped the driver, she walked quickly to the front door and let herself in. Frank trotted ahead of her, just as eager to explore.

"Do you believe this, Frank?" she asked, even though she knew the dog couldn't answer beyond a well-intentioned bark. "This whole place is ours, just us, for two whole weeks."

She bit back a gasp as she took in the interior of the house. She remembered from all the home improvement shows her mom watched that the floor plan here was called "open concept." A vaulted entryway led into a spacious living room, which melded seamlessly into a bright kitchen and dining area. Glass doors opened to a patio with Adirondack chairs and a fire pit.

"This is amazing, Frank." She set her groceries down in the kitchen, pulling the bottle of wine out and placing it on the counter. "Do you see this?"

What truly took her breath away was the view. The lake shimmered just outside, with elegant homes ringing the shore.

"Oh my gosh," she whispered.

Her fingers itched for her camera, wanting to capture the landscape.

A wall of photographs snared her attention. In every one, different happy couples beamed at the camera.

"Huh." She wouldn't have expected any family photographs in a rental house.

She turned away from the pictures to gaze in wonderment at the lake. Oh, yes, she definitely felt inspired. "Oh, wow. Look at this view. Didn't look this big on the website."

Frank, in typical dog fashion, didn't seem all that interested in the scenery. He scurried off, eager to take in all the details of their new temporary home. He made straight for the stairs that led from the foyer to the second floor.

"Frank," Laura called after him. "Come here, Frank."

He didn't listen, most likely too keen to take in all the new smells, and trotted up the stairs.

Carrying her bags, she followed him up to the second story. As she climbed the stairs, she noticed more photos of more couples, all of them looking blissfully happy. *They must have a big family.*

Finally reaching the landing, she trailed after Frank as he poked his nose into a bedroom. Like the rest of the house, it was tastefully furnished, though it lacked a view of the lake.

"Oh, this is nice." She could see herself here, away from her bedroom at home and its childishly yellow-and-pink walls. Yes, she could lie in bed here until late in the morning, letting her mind spin with how she would fill up the hours of her vacation.

Her dog was less impressed, quickly turning and leaving the bedroom.

"What?" she asked, curious about whatever had distracted him.

She followed Frank into another bedroom. Her mouth fell open. It was huge, with a big gorgeous bed where her dog already perched, and—even better—the lake glimmered just outside.

"Oh, wow," she said softly to Frank. "Now *this* is more like it, huh?" With a happy sigh, she sat down on the bed and stroked Frank's silky neck. "Yeah. I think it's exactly what we need."

She couldn't wait to head outside and start taking pictures. At least when she was behind the camera, she didn't feel so adrift.

Fortunately, the car company was able to accommodate Spencer's requests, and the electric vehicle hummed approvingly as he drove to the rental house. He made certain to follow the GPS, sticking to the recommended routes and avoiding any detours. After stopping at a local health food store for some supplies, he got back in the car to hurry to his destination.

Though South Haven had a definite small-town charm, he didn't have time to spend seeing the sights or admiring views. He had to write his dissertation—in only two weeks.

His hands tightened on the wheel as he drove down a tree-lined street. What had he been thinking, putting off writing the most important work of his life? Oh, he'd been assembling a mountain of notecards, all of them covered with his tidy, precise handwriting, but when it came to actually writing the dissertation itself…he'd made no progress. And the defense was just fourteen days away.

Susan had been the one to suggest he try getting out of town. "Maybe you need a place to focus," she'd said when he'd nearly thrown his laptop out the window of his apartment. "Get away from distractions—like me."

"You aren't a distraction," he'd protested, but he hadn't been entirely truthful. She had carefully monitored him whenever he'd sat down to work, reading over his shoulder or making sounds of disapproval when he'd played computer solitaire. She seemed more invested in his dissertation than he was.

Maybe that wasn't fair. She only wanted them to start their future together—two PhDs blazing trails in academia, being a power couple in the field of psychology. Wasn't that what he wanted, too?

*It is*, he told himself. *Stability, security. Finally.*

"Make a U-turn," the GPS said cheerfully.

In her cat carrier in the backseat, Mozart meowed with impatience. She hated car rides.

Spencer cursed softly under his breath as he followed the computer's instructions. He'd been so caught up in his thoughts he'd missed the house, which just went to show how jumbled he was. Hopefully, a couple of weeks of peace and solitude would help him get his head and priorities straight.

He guided the car up the driveway before parking.

Staring through the windshield, he couldn't believe that this amazing house would be his. The woman he'd rented it from had quoted him a price even a graduate student could afford, so he'd jumped at the chance. Lakefront views and total quiet would definitely ensure that he worked.

After getting his luggage from the trunk, he grabbed Mozart's carrier and his canvas bag of groceries, then maneuvered everything to the front door. He unlocked the door and stepped inside. Soaring ceilings and a living room with an enormous fireplace greeted him.

"Wow," he said admiringly, stepping into the open space. "All right, Mozart."

He set her carrier down and opened the latch on the grate. When she gingerly stepped out, he ran an encouraging hand down her back. "This is home for the next two weeks."

Even though she hated car rides, Mozart liked new places. After giving one last assessing look at her environment, she padded off to explore.

He straightened, and his gaze fell on an ice bucket sitting atop the kitchen counter. A bottle of white wine stood chilling in the bucket, and a tumbler waited beside it.

"Well," Spencer said with pleasure, "isn't that thoughtful?" He examined the bottle, recognizing the label. "It's good, too." He picked up the tumbler and saw it was painted with cheerful little daisies. Cute, but not a wineglass. "Deserves a better glass than this."

A hutch held long-stemmed wineglasses, so he set the tumbler down on one of the shelves and plucked a more appropriate vessel for the chardonnay. He brought the glass to the counter and poured himself some wine.

"Here's to a productive two weeks." He raised his glass. It would have been better if someone had been there to toast with him, but that was what this time was about—being alone.

After taking a sip, Spencer put the wine down and went to collect his luggage. It took two trips to bring the three perfectly matched bags up the curved staircase that led to the second floor. Once all his belongings were upstairs, he examined one of the bedrooms. It was a comfortable room with a perfectly pleasant bed, but it wasn't quite what he wanted.

Further investigating uncovered a second, larger bedroom with a bed that faced a spectacular view of the lake. Wonderful. He stacked his bags neatly on the bed and, after ensuring that they were precisely lined up so that they wouldn't topple over, he headed back downstairs. There was just one more thing to do to make the house perfect.

A small pedestal table was exactly the right size and height for his portable phonograph. He took a vinyl

LP out of his canvas bag, then set it carefully on the turntable.

Mozart continued her exploration of the living room, sniffing delicately at the sofa and chairs.

"Hey, Mozart," he said over his shoulder. "How do you like the place?"

He gently lowered the needle onto the record, and immediately the elegant strains of "Spring" from Vivaldi's *The Four Seasons* filled the house. Spencer smiled to himself. He'd spent months tracking down this particular recording of Vivaldi. It had been his mom's favorite.

There was something enchanting about an LP versus a digital recording. It had a warmth and humanity that a download could never achieve. He was glad that he'd taken the chance and brought some of his album collection with him. After he worked all day, he could relax in the evening with Vivaldi, Beethoven, and a few vintage oldies. They reminded him of those rare evenings with his parents, when he'd lie between his mom and dad on the living room floor of his grandparents' house and just listen to music with his eyes closed, sensations of love and belonging enveloping him like an embrace.

The bittersweet memory made his smile fade a little. Maybe someday he could think about his parents without feeling that sense of loss and loneliness.

With the music sweeping through the rooms, he grabbed his wine and ambled down the hallway. If he wasn't mistaken, the description of the house had included a media room. He doubted he'd have time to watch movies, but the film buff in him had to see if the rental came with the latest equipment.

The media room contained four large recliners and a wide-screen television, along with a sizeable assortment of DVDs. Some of them were new releases, but he picked up one that was still in its plastic wrapper.

"*Casablanca.*" He smiled to himself. If he hadn't known any better, he would have thought the rental company had stocked this particular title just for him.

In the distance, a dog barked frantically. He tried to ignore the sound as he perused the rest of the movies. *Singin' in the Rain, Roman Holiday, An Affair to Remember*. The classic romantic films spoke directly to his own personal taste, even though he seldom watched old movies with Susan. She preferred modern, cerebral dramas, and he sat through them dutifully, although they usually left him cold.

The barking grew louder. Spencer looked up from the DVDs when he heard Mozart's annoyed howl. Something thumped and a woman's voice cried out in warning. His heart raced when the unmistakable sound of a record scratching ripped through the noise.

The sounds were coming from inside the house.

Still holding his wineglass, he rushed out of the media room—and immediately collided with someone. Chardonnay went everywhere, including all down his pullover.

Spencer stared down at the elfin blonde woman from the train station, the one with the cute face and annoying dog. She stared back at him in shock.

"You!" he exclaimed.

"You!" she said at the same time. She wiped wine off her shirt, her hands skimming over the camera hanging from her neck.

Mozart leapt up onto the kitchen counter and hissed at the dog, who pawed at the counter and barked frantically.

"What's your dog doing in my house?" Spencer demanded.

"What's your *cat* doing in *my* house?" the woman fired back.

He rushed forward to grab Mozart, cradling her to his body and keeping her away from the excited dog.

"Actually," the woman demanded, "what are *you* doing in my house?"

"That's an easy one. It's not your house. It's mine." He hurried his cat toward her carrier, still waiting in the foyer. "Come on, Mozart. Let's get you somewhere safe—away from that animal."

As he tucked Mozart into her carrier, he heard the

woman say, "He has a name. That's okay," she added softly, presumably for the dog's benefit. "You're not a mean dog. No, you're not. Shh. That's fine, buddy."

Spencer strode back into the living room. The woman had clipped a leash onto the irritating dog's collar. But he barely saw that. All his attention was focused on the phonograph and the record spinning on the turntable.

"Please don't be scratched." Anxiously, he knelt down and took the needle off the record. "Please don't be scratched." His pulse jumped as he examined the LP, terrified at what he might find. "It took me an entire year to find this album."

"Can't you just download it?" the blonde asked with a look that said, *What kind of idiot buys records?*

He glanced at her with annoyed disbelief. "It's not the same. It's like the difference between sunshine and a..." Spencer looked her over. She was just as attractive as she'd been at the train station, except now she gazed at him with exasperation. "A tanning bed."

There were no scratches on the record. He felt himself calm slightly. Standing up, Spencer faced her. "Okay, would you like to tell me what you and your dog are doing here?"

"Look, all I know is I rented this house for spring break. See?" She pulled a piece of paper from her pocket and held it out to him. "I had to fill out this whole questionnaire."

Taking the paper from her, he squinted at it and walked to the kitchen.

"And then I go out to walk my dog," she said, "and I come back, I find you here, drinking my wine. I picked it up on the way here."

His face heated. "Oh. I thought it was a gift from the rental company."

"Nuh-uh," she said as he pulled out his glasses from their case.

He slipped on his spectacles and reviewed the paper she'd given him. From his briefcase on the counter, he pulled out a similar document, except his wasn't wrinkled or covered in feminine cursive, like hers.

"I filled out the same questionnaire," he said, placing his sheet of paper next to her. She glanced at both lists of questions.

"Starting today," she noted.

"Starting today."

"Obviously," she said, "there's been some sort of mistake."

"Obviously. But I don't know how. It was a very personal questionnaire. They seemed to have every other detail covered." When he'd filled it out, it had seemed particularly strange, but he'd shrugged it off and attributed it to the house owner's peculiarities. "I mean, *Favorite Color, Favorite Food, Favorite Movie.*"

"What did you answer for food?" the blonde asked.

"Italian."

She eyed him. "Me, too."

"Favorite movie?" he asked, expecting to hear her name something like *Titanic* or *Bridesmaids.*

"*Casablanca,*" she said without hesitation.

"Me, too."

They stared at each other. Never would he have believed that a woman her age would love that film. But it seemed that she did.

"Well," she said slowly, "maybe they thought we're the same person."

He considered this. "Maybe." It made an appalling kind of sense.

She held out her hand. "Laura Haley."

Spencer lifted an eyebrow. "I'm sorry?"

"If we're going to be stuck in the same boat," she said, "we better know each other's name. Mine's Laura Haley. What's yours?"

"Spencer," he said as he removed his glasses. "Spencer Hodkins." Seeing as how it was the only polite thing to do, he shook her hand.

A current of awareness passed through him when their hands touched.

He shook his head, dismissing it. Clearly, he was

tired and confused. He had a girlfriend, and besides, he'd only just met Laura.

"Well, Spencer Hodkins," she said. "It appears as though we have ourselves a little problem."

# Chapter Three

Laura considered herself a fairly easy-going person. It usually took a lot to light her fuse—like the time Rose had "borrowed" her favorite yellow dress and spilled chocolate sauce *and* red wine on it, then stuffed it into a corner of Laura's closet, hoping it wouldn't be missed. It had taken a whole day for Laura to speak to Rose, and then only after a gift of s'mores.

In that case, Laura had been angry but not permanently so. What mattered was that Rose had been genuinely sorry. Seeing the remorse in her best friend's eyes had wiped away her lingering anger.

There was something about Spencer Hodkins, though, that brought all of Laura's nerves on edge. Maybe it was the way he'd called Frank a "mean dog," when everybody who knew Frank loved him. Or maybe it was the high-handed way Spencer had looked at her when she'd suggested he download that classical music—like she was some kind of airhead.

Or maybe it was the fact that he was undeniably cute, and she wasn't ready right now to find *any* guy cute.

In any case, the sooner he got out of her house, the happier she'd be. He'd sent off an email to the rental company. Now they just had to wait.

While they bided their time, there were more pressing matters to attend to, including feeding a very hungry dog.

"There you go, Frank," she said as she poured kibble into his bowl. "Specialty of the house."

The dog began to eat, blissfully unaware that the source of his owner's irritation sat only ten feet away on a barstool at the kitchen counter. Laura hovered over Frank, more unwilling to get closer to Spencer than she was concerned for her pet's appetite.

A chime sounded from Spencer's laptop, drawing her attention.

"Ah, great," he said. "The rental company just got back to us."

Drawn by curiosity—and definitely not a need to sniff Spencer's woodsy aftershave—she went to stand next to him and look at his computer screen. She *had* to lean close so she could read the email. That was the only reason she got into his personal space.

He read, "'We will…'" He paused and glanced at her before edging back slightly. She pretended not to notice, even though it stung a little. Did she smell like wet dog, or something?

"'We will look into the matter,'" Spencer said, "'and get back to you.'"

"There we go. Problem solved."

He lifted an eyebrow. "That's a little optimistic."

"I'm an optimistic person."

"That's not what I mean," he said as if fighting exasperation. "That's an automated response message. They probably didn't even read my email."

"Maybe you should have been a little more personal," she said. *He thinks he's so smart.* She waved at his laptop. "Here. May I?"

He looked skeptical, but said, "Be my guest."

After pulling the computer closer to her, she began to type, speaking aloud for Spencer's benefit. "'Hi! How are you? I'm fine. I'm *loving* the house you found for me here in South Haven. Now, I don't want to be a bother or anything, but I was wondering if you could help me with a little problem I'm having. You see, there's this man who—'"

Before she could type any more, he tugged the laptop away from her. "Maybe we should just leave it as is."

"I thought you wanted a reply."

"I do," he said in a maddeningly instructive tone, "but it's a psychological fact that people respond better to polite, short exchanges on the internet than to long, drawn-out and weirdly chatty emails."

*Ugh. The nerve of this guy.* "And you're an expert on this?"

He straightened. "I am actually working toward my PhD in psychology right now."

"Oh, really," she said with a hint of sarcasm.

"Really. I'm a TA at my university. I took this place to work on my dissertation."

*That explains why he acts like he knows everything.* She fought to keep from rolling her eyes.

"And what do you do?" he asked like a dad quizzing his kid's friend. "Are you in school?"

"No. I graduated last year. BA in business," she added, just to prove to him that he wasn't the only person with an education.

He appeared mildly impressed. "And now?"

"I'm here visiting my old college roommate and her husband." Laura couldn't wait to tell Rose and Kenny all about Spencer "Too Smart for You" Hodkins. Of course, she'd leave out the part where the graduate student looked like a model for cologne.

"By yourself?" he asked.

"Yeah, why not?" Hopefully he wasn't one of those sexist jerks who thought women shouldn't travel alone.

"I mean, you don't have a boyfriend or…"

Much to her annoyance, he blushed adorably.

"I've got Frank," she said undauntedly.

They both glanced at her dog, who continued to eat without a thought in his head other than an appreciation of kibble. Frank would always be there and would never ask more of her than she was willing to give. Unlike David.

"Huh," Spencer said. "Speaking of, would you mind putting him someplace so I can bring Mozart out for her dinner?"

Laura scowled. "Why can't you go feed Mozart somewhere else?"

He gave a small, disbelieving laugh. "Miss Haley." He closed the laptop. "This is an awkward situation for both of us. Agreed?"

"Agreed," she answered because it was true.

"And the only way we're going to get through this is if we treat each other with dignity and respect. Agreed?"

He had a point. "Agreed."

"That includes respecting each other's pets. Agreed?"

Jeez, he had to be *logical* about it. She tapped her hands on the counter and rose. "Fine. Come on, Frank. Let's go."

Fortunately, her dog had finished his dinner, and

when she motioned for him to follow her, he obeyed. But she wouldn't leave with her own tail between her legs.

"Thank you," Spencer said.

"Oh," she said breezily, "and if we don't hear back from the company in an hour or so, you should probably start calling the hotels around town to find a room." She strolled out of the living room, Frank on her heels.

"Good idea," she heard Spencer say. Then, "Wait, what?"

He was after her in a moment, following her as she and Frank climbed the stairs.

"I'm sure there's someplace you and Mozart can stay the night," she said.

"Wait a minute," he said. "Why am I the one who has to leave?"

Wasn't it obvious? "*Someone* has to."

They reached the landing and she headed toward her bedroom. The door was closed, which she didn't remember doing. Maybe the wind had shut it.

"What are you doing?" he asked when she turned the doorknob.

"You told me to put my dog away." They had just discussed this and he was acting totally weird. She pushed the door open.

"No, not in—"

Frank pushed past her and ran into the room, furiously barking.

"Frank!" Laura was shocked by her dog's behavior—until she heard Mozart's outraged yowl.

She caught a brief glimpse of smoke-colored fur disappearing under the bed. Frank crouched down and continued to bark at the cat.

In an instant, Laura and Spencer dropped to the floor, lying on their stomachs as they peered at the indignant cat.

"It's okay, Mozart," Spencer said in a soothing voice. "He's not going to hurt you."

"He doesn't want to hurt her," she said in a tight voice. "He just wants to play."

"My cat doesn't know that. Could you please just get your dog out of my room?"

If fire could have shot from her eyes, it surely would have at that moment. Furious, she got to her feet. "How is this *your* room?"

He also got to his feet, and she refused to be cowed by the fact that he was a full head taller than her. "I was here first." He waved his hand toward a pile of suitcases so neatly stacked it could have rivaled the most skillfully engineered skyscraper. "See? My luggage."

"Really? How about *my* luggage?" She pointed at her bags at the foot of the bed.

He blinked. "I thought that was laundry."

Her big fabric duffel bag *did* mostly obscure the suitcase beneath it. But still...good grief, this guy really was the worst. There was no way she could talk any kind of sense into him, not when he was so pigheaded.

"Come on, Frank." She hooked her fingers into the dog's collar and led him out the door. "Let's go play with the squeaky squirrel."

As she tugged Frank out into the hallway, she heard Spencer talking to Mozart. "Come on, Mozart," he said in a calming voice. "It's okay, kitty."

She didn't bother to hear the rest of it. Still holding on to Frank, she went down into the living room. She grabbed her dog's favorite toy and used it to distract both Frank and herself. Fortunately, her pet didn't have the best short-term memory because soon he was happily playing tug o' war.

A laugh escaped her. No matter how rough things looked, she could always count on Frank to cheer her up. He entertained her so much she didn't even glare at Spencer when he came back downstairs.

"This whole house mix-up thing doesn't seem to be bothering you very much," he said sourly.

She shrugged, glad that he couldn't see how much he got under her skin. "Yeah, well, there's nothing we can do about it right now. *Que será, será*."

"*Que será, será*," he said doubtfully.

"Whatever will be, will be." She glanced at him. "Like the song. You know—"

"I know where it's from," he said in a snippy voice.

Her jaw firmed. "You don't have to be rude." She refused to look away or let him off the hook. He might be working toward a fancy graduate degree, but that didn't mean he couldn't have some courtesy.

Finally, he nodded. "I'm sorry. It's just, well, I like to plan. And I was planning to have some peace and quiet to get my work done."

"This wasn't exactly what I wanted when I rented the place, either," she said, though she had to sympathize with his desire to focus. She needed some of that in her own life.

"You mean," he said with a rueful smile, "when *I* rented the place."

Oh, if he wanted to be charming… "Fine. You rented the place. I rented the place. So, what are we going to do about it?"

The front door opened and closed, and an attractive woman in her sixties stepped into the foyer. She was dressed in artfully stylish clothes and also wore an apologetic expression.

"Maybe I can help," she said warmly.

Laura cautiously rose to her feet, alarmed by the presence of this stranger. She and Spencer faced the newcomer, almost as if they were a united front. "Hi," she answered slowly. "Who are you?"

"I'm Ellen," the woman explained. "Ellen Davis." She spread her hands out. "I own the place."

"Come in," Laura said. Thank goodness someone was there to take care of the situation. She guided Ellen to the sofa, where they both sat. "We both filled out a questionnaire and a rental agreement, and we both booked the house for the same time. See?" She pulled her crumpled questionnaire from her pocket and motioned for Spencer to show his document to Ellen.

He took the sheet of paper from his briefcase and held it out to Ms. Davis. She slipped on a pair of reading glasses and examined the paper.

Spencer pulled out his cell phone. "I'm going to call hotels and see if they take pets." He paced off, and she heard him talking briskly with someone on the other end.

Ellen winced apologetically. "When I got the text message from the rental company, I came over as soon as I could."

Laura was quick to reassure her. "It's probably just a computer glitch or something."

"That must be it." Ellen nodded. "But..." She grimaced. "The problem remains. I have two tenants, and only one house."

"What about another rental?" Laura suggested.

Ellen shrugged. "I can put in a request for you, but we probably won't hear anything until tomorrow."

Spencer strode back into the room, his phone in his hand. "And none of the hotels in this town take pets," he said with aggravation. "Dogs or cats."

Laura's heart sank. All she wanted was someplace quiet where she could be alone with her camera and her thoughts. A place where she might be able to make sense of the mess that was her life.

How could she do any of that with Professor Perfect breathing down her neck?

"What are we supposed to do?" she asked.

"Right, well, I'll tell you what." Ellen patted her hands on her thighs. "I'm going to waive the first night's rental fee."

Politeness made Laura say, "You don't have to—"

"Thank you," Spencer said, cutting her off. He pasted a smile on his face in clear defiance of the scowl Laura aimed at him. "That's so nice of you."

"And," Ellen said, "I'll check back with you tomorrow. But for now…" She glanced back and forth between them. "I guess it's up to the both of you. So…" The older woman smiled encouragingly. "What do you think? Can you get along for just one night?"

Laura looked at Spencer, and he looked back at

her. She wasn't a PhD candidate in psychology, but she guessed that her dubious expression mirrored his own.

It was going to be a long night.

# Chapter Four

There wasn't much room for debate—Laura had put her bags in the master bedroom first, so, unfortunately, Spencer had to concede the field to her. He'd removed a few items from his luggage and brought them into the smaller bedroom.

"Aren't you forgetting something?" she asked, pointing at his suitcases.

"Maybe by tomorrow, one of us will be gone. I'm just taking the necessities for tonight."

"For all we know, the person leaving tomorrow might be you." She crossed her arms over her chest.

"We'll find out in a few hours."

She scowled, but it didn't make her any less adorable.

He retreated into the smaller room. But it was just

for the night. Hopefully, everything would be sorted out soon.

She wandered off somewhere while he contemplated his clothes. The urge to unpack everything was strong. Whenever he arrived at a new destination, one of the first things he always did was unpack. It gave him that sense of stability and security he craved.

As he took out only the items he'd need for the night and set them carefully in the dresser, he imagined that Laura's version of unpacking was to throw everything on the floor. That kind of messiness would never have been tolerated at his grandparents' home. Since his parents had been off on their adventures, Gram and Gramps had practically raised him, and he'd learned from an early age that an untidy room was frowned upon. He'd never lost the habit.

That made it easier whenever he was over at Susan's spotless apartment. She was just as clean and organized as Spencer, and it would have caused too much friction if he'd walked on her carpet wearing his outside shoes, or left a napkin on the coffee table.

As Mozart watched from the bed, he smoothed his hand over the shirt he'd placed in the dresser. Even if no one was going to see him while he toiled away on his dissertation, he knew he'd never be able to get any work done if he sat around in sweats like some kind of undisciplined slob.

No doubt Laura would just laugh at him if she saw how orderly he needed his person and workspace to be. She probably laughed a lot—when she wasn't being irritated by his presence.

The silence over the house struck him as odd. Had Laura gone out? Maybe she'd abandoned the house completely. He couldn't decide if he liked the idea or if it made him vaguely depressed.

"Want to explore a little, Moz?" he asked the cat.

She blinked at him in response, which he took as a cat version of a yes. Gently, he scooped her up in his arms and left the bedroom. She purred lightly as he carried her downstairs. One of the things he loved about her, and cats in general, was their independence. They took care of their own needs and when they wanted affection, they sought it out with an available human. It was a neat and orderly exchange.

Of course, as a kitten, Mozart had been a little more difficult to anticipate. Spencer had come home from leading a discussion section only to find her crouched atop his kitchen counter, with the vintage salt and pepper shakers lying broken on the floor and a satisfied look on her face. She'd also unraveled an entire roll of paper towels.

As he entered the living room downstairs, he found himself looking for Laura—which, like his fondness for his pet's willful nature, came as a surprise.

He spotted her through the windows. She perched

on one of the Adirondack chairs, aiming her camera at the lake. That was unexpected. He wouldn't have thought she'd have the patience for photography.

For a moment, he considered going back upstairs, or possibly heading to the media room to watch an old movie. Something urged him forward, however, and he headed outside with Mozart still in his arms.

He opened the door leading to the back patio and stepped out cautiously. "Is it safe out here?"

Laura didn't turn around to look at him or even put her camera down. "Frank is upstairs in the bedroom. Asleep." As Spencer stepped out onto the patio, Laura added over her shoulder, "It's not all his fault, you know."

Blaming a dog for human error would be silly, so he said nothing. Instead, he noted the camera in her hands. She seemed comfortable with it. He slowly eased toward her.

"Nice camera," he noted. "My dad had an N90." His mom used to joke that his dad was too busy taking pictures to notice if a bear was attacking. Children weren't allowed on Peace Corps assignments, so between the ages of two and twelve, he'd lived with his grandparents, who would tuck him in at night and read him letters from his mom and dad.

His parents would come back from their Peace Corps assignments with a suitcase full of undeveloped film. After the pictures were processed, they would sit on the grass in his grandparents' backyard and look at all the exotic places his folks had been. Ghana, Mongolia, Nicaragua, Ukraine—places he'd searched for on maps so he knew where to find his parents. Spencer had been both afraid of traveling so far and deeply wistful to visit distant lands with his parents.

The camera had been donated to charity, like most everything, after his dad had passed. Spencer hoped whoever had gotten the Nikon took pictures of happy things, even if no one used film cameras anymore.

"You're a photographer?" he asked Laura now as she snapped another photo.

"Me?" She looked mystified by the idea. "No, not really. I just like to take pictures."

Interesting. "Can I see some?"

She shook her head vigorously. "No. I don't ever show anybody. It's just for me."

*That* got his attention. She seemed uncertain of herself, even though it was clear she enjoyed photography. "Why not?"

The doorbell rang, and she jumped up, almost eager to escape answering his question. "Oh, that's for me," she said as she hurried inside. "I ordered pizza."

"Of course you did," he said to the space she'd occupied. Pizza had been off-limits at his grandparents'. They'd insisted it was junk food fit only to feed desperate animals.

He brought Mozart back inside, just in time to see

Laura carrying a pizza box to the kitchen counter. She opened the lid and he had to stop himself from deeply inhaling the delicious aroma of cheese and bread. *Junk food is a no, remember?*

"Mm," Laura said appreciatively. "Want some?"

He set Mozart down beside her bowl. "No. Thank you," he remembered to add. From the fridge he pulled out some celery stalks. "I'm eating raw this month."

"Hm," she said with a skeptical look. "I don't suppose your cat wants any either?"

"Definitely not," he answered. "*Mozart* is on a very special diet." He glanced at his cat as she nibbled on the expensive hypoallergenic food he'd purchased from the vet. She had allergies, and the wrong kind of food made her itchy and uncomfortable.

"Frank pretty much eats whatever falls on the floor," Laura announced, like it was some kind of badge of honor that her dog was basically a garbage can.

"There you go, then," he said with a shake of his head.

She picked up a slice of pizza. "What do you mean?"

"The difference," he replied. "Between cats and dogs." Cats demanded things to be exactly the way they liked things, and dogs were...undisciplined. Chaotic.

They also lavished unconditional affection on

their owners. Which sounded kind of nice. What would it be like to be the recipient of something's—or some*one*'s—complete, unreserved love?

He realized with an unpleasant sensation in his chest that he didn't know.

Unaware of his thoughts, Laura took a defiantly big bite of pizza. She made a noise of appreciation aimed right at him. "Delicious."

Two could play at that game. He chomped down on a celery stalk. It didn't taste very good, but it was good for him. Still, she didn't need to know that it had the flavor of soap. "Mm, delicious," he said around a mouthful of celery. He made himself smile.

They continued to eat in silence, and despite the fact that the smell of the pizza tempted him, he dutifully chewed his way through celery and carrots. He would do the right thing, even if he didn't like it.

Wanting some space from Spencer and his vegetables of doom, Laura called for an Uber and made the journey across town to Rose and Kenny's house. Her college roommate now lived with her husband in an adorable cottage on a tree-lined street. As Laura stood on the curb, holding Frank's leash, she was struck again with a feeling like being a leaf on a breeze, just wafting around with no direction and no purpose.

It was like her photographs. She loved taking them, loved capturing the mood of a place, but there was nothing special about her pictures. They didn't say anything about her. Anyone could have taken them. She definitely wasn't going to show them to Spencer, who'd probably try to use them to analyze her like a psychology subject.

"Clearly, the person behind the lens needs to get a life," she imagined him saying.

*Not everyone can be Professor Perfect*, she said to herself. *All work and no play.*

*But Rose is happy*, Laura's thoughts reminded her. *She's going somewhere. She's building a life.*

Laura pushed those thoughts down as she approached the front door. It wouldn't be very much fun for Rose if she showed up at her home full of complaints and confusion.

She rang the bell and waited, eager to catch up with Rose and also vent about Spencer. It was more satisfying to complain to a human than to her dog.

The door opened and Laura said, "Hi!" But everything else she'd planned on saying fled when she saw her friend's big, round belly. Rose was pregnant. *Very* pregnant.

"Surprise!" Rose cried, flinging open her arms.

"Oh my God," Laura couldn't help but stammer. "Yeah—surprise. My gosh. Hi." Words of any meaning or significance flew away as she eyed her friend's dramatic change. The paths of their lives veered apart, and Laura felt both happiness and sadness.

"I know," Rose said wryly. But then she hugged Laura, and Laura eagerly returned the hug. Despite Rose's belly poking into her, it felt good to be back in her friend's arms.

They moved into the house. "Your place is so great," Laura exclaimed. She took in the beautiful woodwork and built-ins that made the snug house appear even more adorable. Perfect for a family.

"Is that Loony Laura?" Kenny came out of a room and pulled her in for a hug.

"Is that Crazy Kenny?" she asked with a laugh. He was like the brother she'd never had. They had all been friends in college, but Kenny and Rose had progressed from teasing friendship to marriage. Some people thought that Rose and Kenny had married very young, but it was hard to argue with the love in their eyes whenever they looked at each other.

Rose led her to a couch as Kenny headed into the kitchen. "How do you like your rental? The pictures made it look gorgeous."

"It is," Laura answered. "Except someone else thinks it's gorgeous, too."

"What do you mean?" Rose asked.

She made a face. "There's another tenant. A grad student who brought his cat with him while he works on his dissertation."

"Seriously?" Rose looked appalled. "How does Frank feel about that?"

"You know Frank," Laura said fondly, gazing down at the dog sitting at her feet. "He just wants to play."

Kenny came back into the living room carrying a tray with a teapot and mugs. "Wait, so there's a guy in your place?"

"Yeah," Laura answered. "It's just a mix-up with the rental company. It's fine." She didn't know why she was downplaying the situation. It wasn't like she and Spencer were on friendly terms.

"Why don't you come stay with us?" Rose suggested.

"That's very, very sweet," Laura said at once. "But I've already paid for the house. They're not going to push me out." She'd like to see Spencer try. Hah! She'd just laugh in his handsome face. "Don't worry. It's only for one night, and plus I've got Frank to protect me. Right, Frank?"

He wagged his tail in response and looked at her with adoration. Who didn't like dogs? They were so full of energy and love.

"All right, well," Kenny said, "if you ladies will

excuse me, I've got a nursery that's not going to paint itself."

He bent and kissed Rose. Laura pretended to be interested in her tea rather than remind herself of the fact that she was on her own—again.

Once she and Rose were alone, her friend said brightly as she poured some tea, "I thought you were going to bring David. You guys make such a cute couple."

"Yeah, well," Laura muttered. "Now he's making a cute couple with someone else."

It had been difficult to break up with him, but despite his protests that he wanted to be with her, it hadn't taken him long to find somebody new. Laura had actually spotted David and his current girlfriend at the coffeehouse she and David used to frequent. She'd turned around and gone home, without her favorite iced blended vanilla latte, extra whipped cream.

"Oh, I'm sorry," Rose said.

"No, it's okay." Laura sighed. "It's my fault, mainly. He wanted a commitment and I..." She looked down at her lap. "I just wasn't ready. I feel like I'm not ready for anything."

"What do you mean?"

Laura searched for a way to describe feelings she didn't understand herself. "I mean that..." Thoughts and sensations bumped up against each other. "I've been out of school for over a year and I feel like I'm just lost." She waved at Rose's round stomach. "I see you and Kenny, and you're having a baby. You're getting on with your life. But I'm still at home, working at my parents' accounting business."

She hated how difficult it was for her to simply be elated for Rose, instead of thinking about her own situation. Why couldn't she just be glad for her friend's happiness?

"It's a good job," Rose pointed out, echoing thoughts Laura had already entertained.

"I know," she said. "But it's their job, not mine." She picked up a mug of tea. "I'm just scared that I'm going to wake up some morning and see my mother staring back at me in the mirror."

It wasn't that Laura's mother was a bad person or even a boring one. But her mom was her own person, and Laura wanted to be herself. Whoever that was.

"Okay." Rose nodded. "So what do you want to do with your life?"

"That's just it," Laura answered, barely holding back her frustration. "I have no idea. At all."

Rose looked at her with sympathy, and though Laura knew she could rely on her friend to see her through the toughest times, there were some things a person had to figure out for themselves.

# Chapter Five

Dinner was a solitary affair for Spencer. It was also cold—literally. Eating raw meant finding new and different ways to make vegetables exciting, which wasn't an easy feat. He struggled through lettuce tacos filled with nuts and corn salsa, telling himself the whole time that it was the healthiest option. Last week, he'd read an article that claimed a raw diet increased brainpower, and he needed as much of that as he could get.

"Maybe I should just eat your food, huh, Moz?" he asked his cat as he carried his plate to the sink.

She stared at him as if to say, *You're human. You can eat whatever you want, dummy.*

Just before he turned on the tap to rinse his plate,

his computer on the counter pinged, letting him know that Susan was calling.

He answered the call, and Susan's face appeared on the screen. "Are you in the middle of something?" she asked, eyeing the plate in his hand.

"It can wait."

"We can talk while you clean," she said.

*I guess I'm doing the dishes.* He slung a dishtowel over his shoulder and went to the sink.

"So," Susan said, "how's the house?"

"It's beautiful," he said as he rinsed his plate. "Right on the water. I'm going to get so much work done when they're gone."

"When who's gone?" Susan asked.

*Whoops.* He took his time as he shut off the sink and dried his plate.

"Spencer," she said with that warning tone he recognized as a precursor to an explosion. "I thought you were alone in the house."

"I will be," he said with a false smile. "It's just…the rental company, they messed something up. Double-booked the place."

Was that the front door? If it was, Laura hadn't announced herself. She must have taken Frank right upstairs.

"With who?" Susan pressed.

His mind spun. Obviously, he couldn't tell

his girlfriend that he was sharing a roof with a freewheeling—but pretty—blonde. "It's just this old guy. He's kind of smelly. He's got this mutt, but they'll be gone tomorrow."

Okay, maybe he'd laid it on a little thick, but a harmless little lie never hurt anybody, right?

"Well, that's good," Susan said. She fixed him with a cautioning look. "You really need to concentrate, Spencer. My father is counting on you. And so am I," she added.

As if he needed reminding about the massive pressure he was under. "I know. I will." Hopefully. It would get better once Laura and her dog were gone. No more distractions. "I miss you. Do you miss me?"

Susan looked slightly exasperated by his question. "It's been pretty busy around here—"

Not what he wanted to hear.

"—but of course I do."

He exhaled.

"Good night, Spencer."

"Good night," he answered. Then, trying again when his earlier attempt had failed, he said, "I love—"

She ended the call. Again.

"You," he said to the empty screen. He sighed. So much for having a heartwarming moment. He and Susan had been dating for almost a year, and he'd finally gotten up the courage to tell her that he loved her. But whenever he tried, she found a way to cut him off, and the sentiment was never fully expressed. Was she doing it on purpose? Or maybe she was just so busy focused on getting things done that it was accidental.

Maybe it was better that she wasn't clingy and emotional. They could lead their lives with a minimum of drama.

With Laura, he'd bet there would be a lot of drama. Excitement, too.

He glanced at Mozart, who seemed to look at him with judgment in her golden eyes.

"What?" he asked the cat. "It wasn't exactly a lie." But it totally was.

If he was looking for Mozart to forgive him, he was out of luck. She licked her muzzle as she continued to stare at him.

"Besides," he said as he walked out of the kitchen toward the stairs, "she'll be gone tomorrow. Nobody will ever know, and nobody will get hurt."

His foot connected with something solid and he nearly fell over his suitcases. They were stacked up at the foot of the stairs.

Laura strolled out of the bathroom at the top of the stairs. She wore a bathrobe and was in the middle of brushing her teeth. "Oh!" she said cheerfully. "You found your luggage."

Luggage that he hadn't taken from the master bedroom.

"Yes," he said drily. "Thank you. Good night."

She smirked at him. "Good night." Then she ambled back into the bathroom.

He planted his hands on his hips. So, that was how she wanted to play things. He wasn't a quitter and he didn't back down from challenges. And Laura was definitely a challenge.

Spencer had trained himself to wake up early and get a start on the day. Most people who complained about a lack of productivity were wasting valuable hours by sleeping. Fortunately, Susan fully supported his habit and they often went for a jog almost an hour before the sun came up.

Just because he was here in South Haven didn't mean that he'd abandon his routine.

When his alarm went off at 5:45, he hopped out of bed and threw on his workout clothes. Mozart accompanied him as he headed downstairs with his jump rope and exercise mat.

He quickly began warming up by jumping rope in the living room. The rhythmic movement never failed to clear his mind and get him prepared for the hours ahead.

Only minutes into his workout, Laura appeared, wrapped in a robe and her hair mussed from sleep. She glared at him.

"Morning," he said pleasantly.

"Yeah," she snapped. "It is."

He ignored her sharp tone as he stopped. "I like to get an early jump on the day." He lowered himself down onto the exercise mat.

"At six a.m.?" she demanded.

"Best time to do exercises." He launched into his sit-ups, and her angry face appeared and disappeared whenever he moved to the upright position. "No noises, no distractions. I can work myself into a calm, meditative state."

She looked like she was about to say something highly unpleasant, but before she could speak, Frank appeared at the entrance to the living room. The dog spotted Mozart crouched nearby. He barked and lunged for the cat.

"No, Frank!" Laura shouted.

Mozart sprang to her feet and ran away—right across Spencer's chest. Frank followed, also using Spencer as a highway. Laura chased after both of them, continuing to shout Frank's name as Mozart yowled.

Spencer lay back on the floor with a long,

exasperated exhale. So much for a calm, meditative state. It would be next to impossible to continue to work out with so much chaos around him. He rolled to his feet and went after the parade of human, dog, and cat.

"Easy, Moz," he said when he gathered her up off the fireplace mantel. He eyed Laura, who held a bristling Frank's collar. "Can your pet behave?"

"Can you?" she fired back. Tugging Frank with her, she marched out of the living room and up the stairs. Spencer heard her door bang shut.

He carried Mozart up to his room and put the annoyed cat inside. Once she was secure, he decided he could try to get in a little more exercise. Writing was always easier if he worked out, and he felt the burden of his dissertation crushing him the longer it took him to get down to business.

Jumping rope helped dispel some of his irritation with Laura. She'd looked at him as if he had been busy kicking puppies, not exercising. He didn't know how she stayed so fit, between sleeping in and eating pizza.

Not that he was looking at her figure or anything. No. He certainly wasn't doing that.

Once his workout was done, he headed upstairs and grabbed his toiletries kit and robe. A nice hot shower never failed to settle his thoughts and prepare him for the day ahead.

He walked to the bathroom and tried the door. It was locked. From inside, he heard the sounds of water running. He knocked.

"Just a minute!" Laura said.

But it wasn't a minute. For a full five minutes, he stood there, listening to her brushing her teeth. It sounded like she went over every tooth twice, and then added a third time for good measure. He was also treated to the sounds of her gargling and rinsing.

Finally, just as Spencer was ready to bathe in the kitchen sink, the door opened. Laura emerged in a swirl of humid mist.

She beamed at him, showing off her extremely clean teeth. "All yours." Without a backward glance, she sauntered into her room and closed the door behind her.

Spencer peered into the bathroom. Damp towels were everywhere and the mirrors were fogged. It looked as if an entire sorority had used the bathroom, not one woman.

Even better, only one hand towel remained for him.

With an exasperated grumble, Spencer stalked into the bathroom. He'd just have to make do for now, but this kind of disrespect would not stand. At least it wouldn't last much longer.

After he cleaned up and changed, he went

downstairs to prepare his breakfast. He lined up all the ingredients beside the blender and pulled a few stalks of celery out to chew on while making his smoothie. Sure, it would be more fun to have a croissant or even oatmeal, but he had to stick with his eating plan.

The blender whirred loudly as he pureed his breakfast, sloshing dark purple liquid against the glass.

A dressed Laura wandered in. She stared at the blender like it held a mixture of blood and mud before pulling out the pizza box from the fridge.

It couldn't hurt to be somewhat courteous. "I'm making a kale, beet, celery, vinegar, bark extract smoothie," he said above the whirr of the blender. "Do you want some?"

In response, she grabbed a slice of pizza and held it up as if it was a talisman. "I'm fine, thanks," she replied with a look that said she'd rather literally eat dirt. She took a bite of her pizza and ambled away.

"That's not very good for you, you know," he felt obliged to tell her. She didn't answer, so he bit into his celery, chewing it thoughtfully.

Once breakfast had been consumed, he collected all his supplies needed to work. There was a desk in the living room that looked out onto the water. It would make for a perfect place to write his dissertation, so he approached it without betraying any of the hesitancy that he felt.

Which was silly. A desk couldn't sense fear. It wasn't a horse, for Pete's sake.

He set his mug of herbal tea on the desk and slipped off the strap of his computer bag, placing it on the chair in front of the desk. Something wasn't quite right, though. He took a step back and surveyed the workstation. That was the problem. It wasn't located in exactly the right position.

Spencer tugged the desk slightly away from the window and pulled it three inches to the side. That was better. No—the chair needed to be aligned.

Once that was done, he looked at the top of the desk. Clearly, the lamp situated on top of it was in the wrong place. How could anyone expect him to get anything done when the light wasn't ideal? He nudged the lamp a few inches to the left, then to the right. When he was satisfied with that, he needed to get everything else perfect.

He used a wooden bowl to hold neat stacks of his color-coded notecards. Then he put two tea light candles on the desk. They made the workspace more homey, which would relax him and put him in the right frame of mind for working. Once that was taken care of, he set out his glasses case, ensuring that it was right where he needed it.

Finally, he pulled out his computer and opened it. Sitting down, he put on his glasses. But his muscles felt tight and tense, so he cracked his neck and stretched out his hands so that his fingers were nice and flexible, ready for hours of uninterrupted typing.

The blank document stared at him. He stared back. Any minute now, the words would just flow through him, and he'd channel their brilliance onto the page. Susan and her father expected no less than genius from him, so he had to oblige them.

*Okay, genius, now it's time to actually write something.*

A few thoughts swirled through his head. They gleamed faintly in his imagination, then grew slightly brighter. At last, they seemed to shape into something logical.

His hands hovered over the keyboard, ready to take those thoughts and make them real.

*Here we go.*

Loud, bouncy music pierced the silence. His thoughts ran away like startled geese, never to be corralled again. Spencer whipped off his glasses and looked around. What the heck was that awful racket?

He stood from the desk and followed the sounds. They led him outside, and, naturally, to Laura.

She sat in one of the Adirondack chairs, pointing her camera toward the lake. On the table in front of her was a wireless radio. Frank lay on the other chair, and the dog wagged his tail when Spencer approached.

"Hello," he called above the music. "Can you turn your music down, please?"

She didn't stop taking pictures. "What?"

"The music," he said. "Could you turn it down? I'm trying to write."

"I'm trying to get some inspiration for my photographs." She looked at her viewfinder, then put the camera back up to her eye. It was like he wasn't there.

"Could you use headphones?" he asked.

"No," she said at once. "I don't like them."

Enough. He stepped forward and turned the music down.

Laura shot him a glare.

Summoning his patience, he sat down on the arm of the other chair. "I thought we were going to attempt to get along."

"We were," she said airily, "until you called me smelly. And my dog a mutt."

Had she heard him talking to Susan last night? "How did you—" His ringing cell phone interrupted him. When he glanced at it and saw the caller ID, his stomach unclenched. "At least we're saved," he said to Laura. "It's the rental company. They must have found something by now."

"Oh, good. So you won't be stuck with me anymore," she said, acid in her words.

"And you won't be stuck with me anymore," he replied. He answered the call. "Hello?"

"This is Ahmed from Lakeside Rentals," the voice on the other side of the call said. "Is this Spencer?"

"Yes," he answered, already envisioning a calm, quiet house that was his alone. He smiled.

"We've looked into the situation," Ahmed continued. "Unfortunately, none of our other properties within twenty-five miles are available, and the ones that *are* vacant don't permit pets."

"Uh-huh," Spencer said, the knot returning to his stomach. His smile wavered but he refused to let it go.

"So it looks as though either you and Ms. Haley are going to stay together at the house, or one of you will have to leave."

"Uh-huh." Spencer couldn't think of words beyond those two syllables.

"But we will halve your rental fee," Ahmed added with an attempt at cheerfulness. "And if you book with us again, we'll give you top priority in selecting your next rental property."

"Okay," Spencer said, but all he wanted to do was shout in frustration. "Good."

"We'll be in touch if there's anything else you need," Ahmed continued.

*I need to focus. Can you get me that?* "Very well. Goodbye."

"Have a great day," Ahmed said.

Spencer pressed the button to end the call. Numbly, he slipped the phone into his pocket and stared out at the lake. It reflected the sun like a mirror, totally unconcerned that any hope he'd had of getting his work done had evaporated like so much morning mist.

"Well?" Laura asked from behind her camera.

He planted his hands on his knees. "We're stuck with each other."

She lowered her camera and looked at him with dismay. All he could do was look back at her as the truth set in.

Like it or not, for the next two weeks, Laura Haley was his roommate.

# Chapter Six

*Que será, será.* Whatever will be, will be.

Laura tried to remind herself of this when she heard that she and Spencer weren't parting company anytime soon. She was going to have to make the best of bad circumstances. Stuck in a house with a cute but stuffy guy and his spoiled cat? She could find a way to live with the situation.

"We need to go to the market." She stood from her chair and headed toward the doors leading into the house.

"Why?" He followed her inside.

She set her camera down on the kitchen counter and opened the fridge door. It stood nearly empty. "It might surprise you, but I don't just eat pizza. Sometimes, if I'm feeling really wild and out there, I occasionally even eat a vegetable." Closing the door, she faced him. "But unlike you, I believe in this crazy idea called *cooking*."

"I'm just eating raw for the month," he protested.

"Right. Because four weeks of cold food when a perfectly good microwave is available makes total sense."

He crossed his arms over his chest. "Studies have shown that heating your food robs it of vital nutrients and natural enzymes. We need those enzymes to help digestion and fight disease."

She shook her head. "You sound like you're reciting a pamphlet someone hands out at the health food store."

"I've got my reasons for choosing to live my life the way I do," he said stiffly. "Just like you have your reasons for…" He waved his hand as if indicating her whole chaotic existence. "For whatever it is that you do."

She raised an eyebrow. He had a point—she knew almost nothing about him, just like he knew almost nothing about her. You couldn't judge somebody based on a handful of random observations.

"Fine," she said after a minute. "I'm going to assume that the electric car in the driveway is your rental."

"Why assume that?"

"Because it's practical and smart—just like you."

He looked stunned. “Did you just say something nice to me?”

She grinned. “Don’t get used to it.”

“Believe me, I won’t.” He grabbed his keys and started walking toward the front door. “I’ll drive.”

“You don’t trust me to drive?” She picked up her purse and followed him.

“First of all,” he said as he unlocked the car, “your name isn’t on the rental agreement, so if we got in an accident, it would be a complete mess.” They climbed into the car at the same time. The first thing he did was fasten his seat belt.

She adjusted her seat, then checked her reflection in the mirror on the visor. At least she’d remembered to put on mascara and lip gloss today, even if it was supposed to be a vacation. Drat—having Spencer around meant she’d have to put her makeup on before setting foot outside of her room. There was no way she wanted him to see her without her game face.

“The second thing?” She buckled her seat belt.

He checked the rearview and side mirrors before turning the car on. Slowly, deliberately, he backed the car out of the driveway. “I get the feeling that driving with you is like riding shotgun during the Indy 500.”

“I’ll have you know that I passed my driver’s test the first time I took it.” She sniffed. “And nobody had to wear a helmet.”

Of course, she couldn’t be blamed if, when she was

alone on the road, she liked to test the speed of her dad's midsized sedan. But Spencer didn't need to know that, and neither did her dad.

She and Spencer drove together without speaking, with the public radio DJ filling in the silence with a report about the rise in raw food diets.

"See?" Spencer pointed to the radio. "I'm not setting any precedents."

"Yeah, but if you listen to the guy on the radio, he's saying that the health benefits from not cooking your food haven't been proven."

"Nobody wanted to believe Galileo, either."

"Chugging wheat grass instead of eating a scone is not the same as proving the Earth revolved around the sun." She smirked at the surprise on his face. The professor didn't think she knew who Galileo was.

Spencer snapped off the radio, and neither spoke for the rest of the journey. As she'd expected, he was a very careful driver, checking several times before making a lane change and flipping on his turn signal a full block before turning.

He stopped at a crosswalk to let a father and his young son cross the road. The dad held his son's hand as the little boy toddled beside him. Laura chanced a glance at Spencer as he watched the progress of the parent and child. He frowned slightly, as if trying to understand a complex equation.

"You planning on kids someday?" Laura heard herself ask.

Spencer blinked as if waking up. Once the crosswalk was clear, he drove on. "I haven't thought about it yet. What about you?"

She snorted. Her? In charge of someone else's life? "I need to get some stuff sorted out before I can take that leap."

"It's a big responsibility. Some people need to think clearly before taking it on." He said this like someone who took that responsibility very seriously—someone who spoke from experience.

Before she could ask him what he meant by that, he pulled into the parking lot of the market.

Inside, he got a cart and they walked down the aisle together. The shop wasn't like the giant supermarkets in her suburban home. It was quaintly arranged with farmstand-like displays of produce, a yummy-looking selection of fresh bread, and jars of what looked like homemade jam lined up on cupboard shelves. A sign read, "If you ate today, thank a farmer," which made her smile.

As they walked, he said, "I guess the best way to do this is for both of us to submit our respective meal plans and then divide up the cost of groceries." He picked up a bunch of bananas and, after inspecting them, placed the fruit in the cart.

"Meal plans?" She looked at him, baffled.

"You just decide what you want for breakfast, lunch, and dinner for the coming week and then you shop accordingly."

Laura stopped walking and stared at him. He couldn't be for real. "Are you kidding? I never plan that far in advance." Which explained a little as to why she still lived at home.

"It's not that difficult." He picked up a watermelon and gave it an experimental thump. It figured that he approached picking food with the same deliberate care as he drove. "You just make a choice and stick with it." Gently, he set the watermelon in the shopping cart.

"What if I decide on chicken wings for Thursday and then by Wednesday I change my mind and want macaroni and cheese?" She looked up at him. "Then I'm stuck."

He appeared just as puzzled by her as she was by him. "You can't just order pizza every day."

"I don't. Sometimes I get Chinese, or Mexican, or Thai."

"That's not exactly a healthy way to live," he said as he investigated the carrots.

There was just no way to get through to Professor Perfect. "Okay, fine," she said like she accepted his challenge. "I'm going to get groceries."

He didn't look up from his perusal of the

vegetables. Naturally, he'd find carrots more worthy of his attention than the actual human being standing beside him. "Good."

She broke away from him and walked purposefully toward a display she'd spotted on her way into the market. She gathered up what she wanted and brought it back to where he stood with the cart.

"Graham crackers," he said, eyeing her groceries as she set them down. "Marshmallows and a chocolate bar." Spencer stared at her in disbelief. "That's what you're going to eat?"

For a moment, all she could do was look at him as if he was a Martian. "You're kidding, right?"

He frowned. "About what?"

"You've never had s'mores before." She couldn't believe she was having this conversation. "You take the chocolate and then you melt it with the marshmallow—"

"I know what s'mores are, thank you. I just choose not to put that much sugar and whatever other chemicals are in that"—he gestured toward the pile of her items in the cart—"into my body."

Naturally. Because heaven forbid he could let loose for even a second. She wanted to ruffle his neatly combed hair just to see what he'd do. "Well, I do."

The rest of the shopping trip was a study in contrasts. She loaded up on frozen food and instant soup while he very thoroughly examined every inch of the produce aisle. Judging from the stuff he put on the cash register conveyor belt, eating raw meant a lot of seaweed and sprouts. No thank you; she'd take packaged ramen and fish sticks over that stomachache waiting to happen.

As they drove home, past the waterfront, she stared out the window. "This place is so gorgeous."

"Thinking about taking pictures?" he asked with a smile.

"There's no shortage of subject matter, that's for sure," she said. "Does the scenery inspire you?"

He chuckled. "I'm all about science and facts. Scenery has nothing to do with my work."

"That's a shame."

His forehead scrunched. "Why?"

"Because what's the point of being alive if you can't take in all this?" She waved at a dozen birds flying in formation.

"Maybe it's about making the world a better place than you found it. Maybe it's about contributing something to society."

She studied him. He was a lot deeper than she'd given him credit for. If only he could learn to ease up on the brakes—both metaphorical and literal—once in a while, he might actually be an interesting person to get to know.

They arrived back at the house and went inside with their groceries. He carried a canvas bag containing the majority of the produce department, while she held a paper sack that, in comparison, looked like a ten-year-old had gone on a grocery shopping spree.

"Tell me about this paper you're writing," she said as they set their bags on the counter.

"My dissertation?" He seemed confused by her interest. "I don't think you'd be very interested in that."

"Try me." She pulled a frozen cheesecake from her bag.

"Okay," he said. "You know much about psychology?"

"I've got two slightly overbearing parents. Does that count?"

He laughed, and it was a nice sound. Too bad he didn't do it more.

"I'm presenting a paper on psychobiology," he explained as he pulled more celery out of his canvas sack, "specifically as it relates to human emotion."

"Kind of like how the taste of pizza makes me happy?" She was only half kidding.

"Not exactly." He opened the fridge and neatly stacked his produce in the bins. "My theory is that any strong emotion like love or heartbreak is nothing more than a series of chemical reactions in the brain."

Jeez. That didn't sound like fun at all. "You sound just like my father. He reduces everything to numbers." Her dad had once even made a graph showing which of her mom's Christmas cookies he liked best, on a scale of one to ten.

"He's not wrong," Spencer said. "When we talk about connecting with someone, all we really mean is that *their* neural biochemistry in some way influences *our* neural biochemistry, resulting in a reaction that people call love."

Laura frowned. What a depressing, clinical view of something that defied science and logic. "Have you ever been in love, Mr. Hodkins?"

"Matter of fact," he said, "I have a girlfriend. Her name is Susan."

"Oh." That was…not expected. And it didn't sit well with Laura. But it explained who he had been talking to on the computer last night.

She found herself bothered by his response, but she didn't know why. Naturally, Spencer had had a life before he came to South Haven. That life would continue once he left. She and Spencer would part ways and probably never see each other again—which was fine. It really was.

"Are you in love with Susan?"

Why had she asked him that? She didn't care!

"We're in a relationship," he said slowly. As if that explained everything.

"It just sounds more like a science experiment to me." She finished unpacking her groceries, but before she left the kitchen, she threw over her shoulder, "Are you sure that she's happy?"

She didn't wait to hear his answer.

Laura's question haunted Spencer for the rest of the day. He wasn't sure how to answer her, and that bothered him. Surely Susan was happy being in a relationship with him. They liked all the same things. They read the same books and ate at the same vegan café three days a week. She was a graduate student in psychology, just like him. Similarities meant little friction. That was enough to build a relationship on, wasn't it?

And if he sometimes wished they could be a little more spontaneous—like trying the Ethiopian restaurant rather than going back to the vegan café, or putting down their books and going sailing on Lake Michigan instead—well, he could handle that. Relationships were a series of compromises. No one got everything they wanted. Her neurochemistry and his neurochemistry matched. That had to be adequate.

That night, when Laura had macaroni and cheese

with fish sticks for dinner, he barely resisted asking her for a bite. Instead, he ate nearly a haystack-sized pile of kale topped with raw pumpkin seeds, trying to distract himself from his meal by reading the latest monograph about the psychology of bonding in primates.

With Frank and Mozart sleeping upstairs in their respective bedrooms, Laura went outside into the chilly spring evening with her s'mores supplies and, to his amazement, deftly lit a blaze in the fire pit. Instead of reading, he watched her through the glass for a long time. He couldn't understand how she just went about her business with no plans for tomorrow or the days after that. It had to be terrifying. Yet she didn't seem scared at all. If anything, she appeared baffled by his sticking to rules and schedules.

It must be kind of nice to be so uninhibited. He had never gotten the chance to experience that kind of freedom.

Grandpa had liked routine, so every week, the meals followed a set pattern. Meatloaf on Mondays, chicken and potatoes on Tuesday, and so on. And when it came to Spencer, both Grandma and Grandpa said he had to come home right after school and do his homework—no television until after dinner. Even then, he could only watch PBS for an hour before being sent to bed. Every hour had been accounted for.

Spencer had kept that kind of routine when he'd

gone away to college, and again when he'd become a graduate student. It felt familiar and comfortable. There was no need to change. Susan told him she liked his predictability because she always knew what to expect. He would never surprise or shock her.

Abruptly, he set his book aside. There'd be time for reading later. Right now, he wanted to experience what it was like to sit next to a fire beside a lake. Having Laura as company might be a bonus.

After grabbing a throw from the couch, he went outside. The air held a bite, but it wasn't unpleasant. A big, full moon hung in the night sky, shining down with an almost magical light.

"It's cold out here," he said to Laura. "You want a blanket?"

"Sure, thanks." She took it from him and draped it over her lap.

He noticed that she'd taken her graham crackers, marshmallows, and chocolate and put them to use, holding a little sandwich in her hand. "S'mores, huh?"

"Want to try one?" She held it out invitingly as he sat in the chair beside her.

"I told you I don't do sugar."

Her smile was impish. "I promise I won't tell anybody."

"All right." After a moment, he took the s'more from her and held it gingerly. The marshmallow oozed out the sides, which made it impossible to keep his fingers clean. He could almost hear Susan sighing in exasperation. That was when he decided to take a bite.

Gooey sweetness filled his mouth along with the crunch from the graham crackers. It tasted like…fun. In a little edible package.

"You know," he said with surprise, "it's actually pretty good."

She laughed, and he liked how easily the sound came to her. "Didn't you ever have a campfire as a kid?"

He barely remembered the cramped flat his parents had lived in before they had gone, leaving him with his grandparents. "I'm fairly certain it was against the law in my apartment building." Given that his granddad was a retired firefighter, the last thing Grandpa wanted in his backyard was a fire.

Spencer and Laura chuckled together. It felt nice. Much better than when they'd been going at each other's throats.

"Every summer," she said wistfully, "my parents and I would go camping for a week. It was the most fun we'd have all year. Actually," she added in a wry voice, "it was kind of the *only* fun that we would have all year."

"It was that bad, huh?" He looked at her with sympathy.

"Almost." She sighed. "They're both accountants, so they do everything by the book."

*Now* she was beginning to make sense to him. "And that's why you don't."

She looked rueful. "Don't get me wrong. I love my parents."

"But…"

"But…" She contemplated the marshmallow she'd stuck on the end of a stick. "I don't want to turn into them."

He gave her an ironic smile. "Some people say we all turn into our parents eventually."

She looked horrified. "Thanks. Now I feel *so* much better."

"I said 'some people.'"

When they laughed together again, he leaned into the sensation. She was actually very easy to talk to, and the firelight shined in her eyes when she smiled.

He slipped into thoughtfulness. Perhaps he could convince Susan to come out with him to the shore some night. They could light a bonfire, and maybe he might even convince her to try a s'more. Though he doubted she'd go for it. Susan's mom had diabetes, and as a result, Susan avoided sugar as much as possible.

Ideas swirled around in his head, struggling to form into words. Strangely, he had a feeling that whatever he said to Laura now, she wouldn't laugh at him or say something cutting. She had a genuineness that he seldom encountered.

"I think it's more like…" He struggled to find the right words. "Being on the water. Your parents, they give you a boat. Maybe it's a raft, maybe it's a yacht." He'd definitely had a raft, and a leaky one, at that. "But then it's up to you to decide where you're going to steer it."

Laura didn't sneer at him. She actually thought about what he said, and when she spoke, her words were contemplative. "What if we don't know where we want to go?"

Did she speak from experience? "I think, deep down, people know where they want to go. They're just afraid to admit it."

She looked at him pensively, but her expression shifted into one that was almost warm—like she hadn't expected him to have these kinds of thoughts.

Perhaps they were different from who they believed each other to be.

"Sorry for that crack about you and your girlfriend," she said. "It wasn't fair. I apologize."

That was surprising. "Apology accepted." He exhaled. "Truth is, you might not be too wrong." It shook him to think so, but he hadn't been able to get past the idea that Susan wasn't happy, and maybe there was something more to be had in a relationship besides neurochemical compatibility.

"How your parents did everything by the book?" His breath misted in the cool night air.

"Mine—they didn't even read it."

He gave a small, wry laugh, and she joined him. Something occurred to him, urged on by Laura's insight. "I guess I was drawn to psychology as a way of finding out the answers to the questions I always wanted to ask them."

She didn't try to say something that might fix it or make it better. She only nodded in understanding, and that quiet act of compassion was all he needed.

"Do you think we try so fiercely not to become our parents that we go too far?" she asked after a moment. "Like, maybe the pendulum swings hard in the other direction, and instead of making everything better, it just makes our lives more difficult?"

He thought about this. "That's a good theory. But then everybody is doomed to go in one direction or the other, and never find their own path."

"Ugh." She propped her chin in her hand. "What a depressing thought."

"Just elaborating on your theory."

"Maybe we should talk about something else," she suggested. "Something less gloomy."

"Hm." He scratched his chin. "How long have you had Frank?"

She immediately perked up. "I got him my senior year of college. Rose and I lived in an apartment complex that allowed dogs, so I went to the local animal shelter and found him waiting for me." She laughed. "I walked by all the cages, and Frank stuck his nose out from between the bars to lick my hand. He had this look on his face like, *You're my human.* I knew then that we were meant to be together."

"Dogs are a lot of responsibility," Spencer said.

Laura lifted an eyebrow. "And I'm not a responsible person. Is that what you mean?"

He raised his hands in a calming gesture. "I didn't say that."

"But you implied it."

"You're the one who can't make a grocery list," he said.

She heaved a sigh. "Yeah. That's true. In that context, I guess it doesn't make sense for me to run out and get a dog. But…" She poked at the fire with her stick. "I think I wanted to care about someone else. Someone who loved me just as I am, and I didn't have to change to make him happy." Laura pursed her lips. "Maybe that's selfish."

"I don't think so," Spencer said. "It sounds…nice."

"It is. And when I feel like I can't figure out how

to put one foot in front of the other, I remember that before I can do anything, I need to take care of Frank."

"He grounds you."

A corner of her mouth turned up. "I guess he does. What about you and Mozart? Aren't cats a little impulsive?"

"Because I'm the opposite of impulsive?"

"If the kale smoothie fits..." She shrugged.

He gazed into the fire. "I didn't plan on having any pets. My grandma was allergic to everything with fur. I could have gotten a lizard or a bird, but I hated the idea of keeping anything in a cage."

Laura's smile was gentle. "That's considerate."

"I found Mozart by a recycling bin near my apartment," he went on. "She was just a kitten. The graduate student apartments didn't allow cats, but I snuck her in under my sweater. I managed to keep her a secret for a month before the building manager found out, and by then, there was no way I was going to give her up. So I had to find a new apartment."

Laura pressed her fingers to her mouth. "Oh my gosh, that is the cutest thing I've ever heard. You, with a tiny kitten under your sweater? I'm totally dead." She pretended to faint.

He chuckled. "That's why I can travel with Mozart instead of leaving her at home. She's pretty fearless in new situations."

"And is her daddy also fearless?" Laura asked.

His laugh turned self-deprecating. "Hardly. I guess it's good one of us is, even if she is only a cat."

"Maybe courage is something we teach ourselves," she said.

"You're Miss *Que será, será*," he pointed out. "Must be pretty brave."

"I don't know if it's bravery or foolishness."

"Is there a difference?" he asked.

"Ask me in five years," she said. "Or better yet, don't ask me. Because I honestly have no idea where I'm going to be." She eyed him. "I bet you know exactly where you'll wind up five years from now."

He opened his mouth to deny it but found he couldn't. Everything in his life had been completely thought out, down to when he'd get tenure at a university and how old he planned to be when he finally retired. "Guilty."

"That sounds comforting. Nothing left to chance."

"You don't think I'm being boring and predictable?"

"It beats whizzing around the universe like an escaped balloon." She got to her feet and stretched as she yawned. "Time for bed. I'm wiped out because I had planned on sleeping in this morning, but something woke me at six."

He winced but said, "You could join me, you know. Exercise is great for creativity."

She ambled to the patio door. "As soon as I know someone with creativity, I'll let them know. Good night, Spencer." She went inside, shutting the door behind her.

He frowned at her last comment. She clearly didn't have much confidence in her ability as a photographer, which seemed too bad.

Her lack of self-assurance wasn't his problem, but as he watched the fire in the fire pit slowly extinguish itself, he realized that he'd learned a lot about Laura Haley tonight. In fact, he'd learned a lot about both of them, and what he'd discovered made him question whether or not people were merely a collection of chemical reactions—or if they were much more mysterious and complex than he'd believed.

# Chapter Seven

The next day, Laura walked with Frank to meet Rose at a café so they could plan the baby shower, but she couldn't stop thinking about last night's surprising conversation with Spencer. Not only had he tried the s'more and discovered he actually liked it, but he'd been thoughtful and understanding when they had talked about their families. All of their conversation had given her plenty to think about.

It would have been so much easier if Spencer had been merely some uptight and snobby graduate student, but he'd revealed so much more about himself, she had to reconsider her opinion of him.

Spencer Hodkins was actually a good, thoughtful person. Granted, he hid behind an image of dreary perfectionism, but that core of kindheartedness was there.

She ambled to the café, letting Frank sniff at whatever caught his interest and making sure she gave herself enough time to meet Rose for their 12:30 lunch date. She had brought her camera with her, just in case something caught her eye, and she took a few pictures of streetlights and storefronts.

Turning onto the main street, she strolled and looked in shop windows. One boutique had a cute display of dresses for the upcoming summer, and she stopped to look at them. A long, flowing dress covered with bright flowers caught her eye.

Of course, wearing a fun outfit like that presumed that she had somewhere to go and someone to go there with her.

"At the rate my personal life is going," she said to Frank, who was looking up at her, "I'd be lucky if you drooled on my dress as a sign of your approval."

Frank yipped in response before turning his attention to a crack in the sidewalk. Laura looked back at the sundress.

*Would Spencer like seeing me in this outfit?*

*Oh my gosh,* she thought at once, *who cares?* Spencer wasn't her boyfriend. Heck, he wasn't even her friend—just some random handsome guy she happened to be stuck with for the next two weeks.

Although… Last night had taken them dangerously close to friend territory.

She and Frank moved away from the boutique window and continued on toward the café. Unfortunately, the shop windows didn't fully distract her, and she kept thinking about what Spencer had said about his family, and why he'd gone into his field.

*I guess I was drawn to psychology as a way of finding the answers to the questions I always wanted to ask them.*

Why couldn't he ask his parents now? Maybe they weren't in his life. Or maybe they had passed away. Either way, it meant that he was traveling through life basically on his own. Her parents did drive her crazy, but she knew they loved her and that they'd be there for her. Perhaps Spencer didn't have the same kind of support.

She felt a squeeze of sympathy in her chest. It made sense why he wanted to reduce everything, especially love, to chemical reactions. Science was predictable and controllable, even when the heart wasn't.

Goodness knew that when it came to what *her* heart wanted, she couldn't figure it out.

The café was just ahead, so Laura pushed away her brooding thoughts. After tying Frank to a lamppost, she entered the restaurant wearing a big smile for her friend. Rose waited at a table in the window. Clearly, her friend had been shopping, because she was surrounded by colorful bags.

"Thanks for getting away from Cat Guy long enough to meet me." Rose carefully got to her feet and hugged Laura, who returned the hug. They sat and looked over the menus.

"He's too busy polishing his glasses and dusting his desk for the eighth time to notice that I'm gone." That wasn't entirely fair to Spencer, and Laura immediately regretted making a joke at his expense. "Actually, it's not bad. When he isn't trying to pick my brain apart, he's a pretty decent guy."

Rose lifted one eyebrow. "Really?"

"Really." The things Spencer had revealed to Laura last night were private, so she didn't elaborate.

She and Rose both ordered salads and iced tea—a far cry from the tater tots and frozen enchiladas they'd devoured back in college—and when the waiter left, Rose pulled out a notebook.

"You're taking notes?" Laura looked at her friend with disbelief.

"To plan the shower," Rose said. "I've got to think about so many things: food, drinks, entertainment, decorations. And that doesn't even include figuring out the guest list."

Laura picked at a roll in a napkin-lined basket. "Who's going to be there?"

"You, of course. Kenny's mom and sister. Some friends from work. Mrs. Woods, who's the office administrator." Rose rolled her eyes. "She's always giving me a hard time about using the copier too much."

"Why invite her?"

"Because if I didn't, she'd revoke my copier privileges completely."

Laura and Rose giggled at that. It was so strange to hear Rose, who had loved going to Mexico for crazy spring breaks, talk about regularly using a photocopier.

The waiter brought their drinks and food. "Is there anything else I can get you?" he asked.

"Ten thousand dollars and an army of house elves to do my bidding," Rose answered.

"I'll see what I can do about that," the waiter said without missing a beat. "Enjoy your lunch."

Once he'd gone, Laura and Rose began to eat.

"I didn't expect you to order a salad," Rose said, eyeing Laura's food.

"Me, either." Laura poked at the lettuce and cucumbers artfully arranged on her plate.

"Aren't you the one who eats nothing but tuna melts and cheeseburgers for lunch?"

Laura shrugged. "Fresh vegetables just sounded nice." Maybe Spencer's healthy habits were rubbing off on her. Not everything. He'd still wakened her at six in the morning with his jump rope. Maybe she could hide it or burn the darned thing.

After a few bites, Rose picked up her notebook and scanned it. "Who knew a baby shower would take so much organizing? How am I going to fit all of these people into our little house?"

Laura smiled at her friend. "I'm just so happy for both of you." She meant it, too. Still, she shook her head and chuckled. "Wild Rose. Who would have thought?"

"I know, right?" Rose looked just as mystified as Laura by the change. "It had been on our minds for a while. And then Kenny got a new job and we bought the place, so the timing just made sense."

"This is not the Rose that I remember from college. We never used to plan anything."

"Yeah," her friend said. She swirled the iced tea around in her glass. "I just got kind of tired of never knowing what's next."

Clearly, Rose had some kind of magic mirror that showed her scenes from Laura's life, because her comment hit Laura dead-on. Once again, she was struck by this feeling of floating around aimlessly while others moved with direction and purpose through their lives. They had goals. Laura had...nothing.

"What about our theme song?" Laura asked. "*Que será, será*?"

"I guess I just finally figured out what I want."

Laura sighed wistfully. "I wish I could do that." It was hard not to feel envious of Rose and the focus she had. "I just...I don't know...I don't see myself settling down anytime soon."

Rose looked at her warmly. "Trust me, when you meet the right guy, it's not going to feel like you're settling down at all." She gave a small, private smile as if thinking about a particular memory of her and Kenny. "It's going to feel like you're starting the biggest adventure of your life." Her eyes suddenly widened. "Balloons! I forgot the balloons!"

Laura watched Rose frantically scribble down a note for the important balloons, but her thoughts wandered. Getting into a relationship now, when she was so uncertain of what she wanted for herself, wasn't a good idea. Maybe she did long for someone to do things with. Someone to laugh with and eat s'mores with in front of a fire.

But she had to get her head out of the clouds before she could even consider something as complicated as love.

With Laura and Frank out of the house, Spencer let Mozart roam while he worked on his dissertation. He'd eaten a sensible lunch and sat himself down at the desk in the living room, where he had set up his computer and research materials.

Now was the perfect time to get some writing

done. No blond-haired, bubbly distractions. No dog drama. Just quiet and work.

He stared at the screen in front of him. For thirty minutes, it read the exact same thing:

> THE CHEMISTRY OF LOVE: Psychology and Human Emotion
>
> By Spencer Hodkins

The cursor blinked as his fingers hovered over the keyboard. After a moment, he lowered his hands and used the chamois to clean his glasses. Once they were spotless, he very deliberately returned the scrap of fabric to the glasses case.

No wonder he couldn't concentrate—his note cards weren't perfectly stacked on top of each other. He straightened each pile, making sure they were exactly where he wanted them.

*Okay, time to get down to business.*

But words simply refused to flow. They crowded his brain but had no way to come out.

He looked up from his screen to stare at the lake. It shimmered like a mirror, and he found himself gazing at the water's surface as if it held the secret to why he couldn't seem to make himself work. Nearby trees swayed gently in the breeze.

Maybe if he went outside and got a little fresh air, it might help clear his mind.

He got up from his desk and stepped out onto the patio where he and Laura had sat last night. It was a pleasant spot, with a pergola overhead, and he stood next to the Adirondack chairs as he looked at the lake.

It was too bad Laura had gone out. He could use some company right now, and talking with her might take his mind off the fact that he'd written exactly eleven words in the last half hour.

*Maybe you need to think less and live more*, he imagined her saying.

His restless gaze fell on the small radio she'd left out on a nearby table. After glancing around to make sure he was alone, he turned the radio on and turned the volume up.

Jangly, upbeat pop music filled the air. It wasn't exactly the kind of music he liked, but still, it made his toes tap in time with the beat. The cheerful music reminded him a lot of Laura. It seemed light and frothy at first, but it held a surprising depth.

As the music played, his body urged him to move. He found himself bobbing along with the song. It didn't quite qualify as dancing, but it felt good to move around after sitting fruitlessly at his desk.

With the music turned up, he almost missed the chime of his computer inside indicating that someone was calling him. Quickly, he shut off the music and ran inside.

He stumbled on something lying on the ground. Picking it up, he saw it was Frank's squeaky squirrel toy. He carried it with him to his desk, and, after setting it down, he answered the call.

A concerned-looking Susan appeared on the screen. "Spencer. Where were you?"

"Just getting some fresh air." He sat down so he could turn his full attention to her.

"Be careful," Susan said. "There's a lot of pollen this time of year."

"Of course," he answered at once. Every day, Susan looked up the pollen count to make sure neither she nor Spencer suffered from any allergies. He didn't want to mention that he'd never had allergies, and neither did she, but it paid to be cautious just in case.

"Is the old man gone yet?" she asked.

He blinked at her. "Huh?"

"The old man, and his dog."

How could he have forgotten that he hadn't told Susan the truth about Laura? "Oh, right. Yeah," he said with a nod, "gone. Place is empty. Just me," he added.

She looked relieved. "Well, that's good. You don't need any distractions."

"Absolutely." Telling her that he'd been blocked for

days would only make things worse. She'd get worried and say again that she and her father were counting on him, which didn't make Spencer feel any better.

"How's it going?"

His thoughts were so jumbled, all he could do was ask, "Hm?"

"Your paper." She laughed as if she couldn't believe he'd forgotten something so important. "How's it going?"

"Oh. Good. Yeah—fine. You know, it's coming along." Coming along exactly from no place to nowhere.

"I can't wait to read it," she said.

He couldn't either. But that presumed that it was going to be written. Silence fell, and then Spencer heard himself ask, "Uh, Susan?"

"Yes?"

*Just say it.* "Are you happy?"

She looked confused by his question. "What do you mean?"

"Are you happy?" He leaned closer to the screen, and his heart beat faster as he searched for her answer. "With us. With me."

Susan's face shifted into that expression he'd seen her use whenever she humored him. "Don't be ridiculous, Spencer."

His heart sank, but he didn't know why he'd hoped

for more from her. One of the principal attractions of their relationship was how rational and steady it was, with no wildly fluctuating sentiments or feelings.

"I've got to go," Susan said. "I've got that fundraiser. I'll call you later."

"Okay," he said. "Love—"

The call disconnected.

"You," he said to his reflection on the screen. Maybe it was time to stop saying something that he knew would never be repeated back to him.

He looked over at Mozart, who had crept into the room and sat herself down near the desk. She gazed at him, her gold eyes full of judgment at his lies.

"Stop looking at me like that," he said to the cat. "There's no reason for Susan to find out. And it's not like we're doing anything wrong."

His pet seemed unmoved by his rationale.

Frustrated, he tapped his hands on the desk. His fingers encountered the plush fur of Frank's squirrel toy.

He and Laura were so unalike in so many ways. Completely incompatible. Sharing a roof with her was going to be thorny, especially because he struggled to write a single word, and she wasn't even home right now.

An idea hit Spencer, and he deleted all eleven words he'd written that day. But soon, new words filled the screen, and he smiled with satisfaction.

# Chapter Eight

After lunch was over, Rose hurried out the door to an appointment with a caterer for the shower.

"I can go with you," Laura offered. "I'm really good at eating."

Her friend smiled. "Thanks, but it's just going to be me and Imani going over price lists and head counts. It'll be super boring. No," Rose added as she hefted herself to standing, "the day is so gorgeous. You should take Frank and that camera of yours and do some exploring."

So Laura found herself strolling through South Haven, her camera in one hand and Frank's leash in the other. It was a short distance from the café to a lakeside boardwalk, and a fresh breeze blew in off the water. Energized by her surroundings, Laura snapped a few shots—the pier, a seagull, more water birds, train tracks that had long been out of use. There was just so much more here to capture than in the bland, boring Lansing suburb she called home.

Frank tugged on his leash, and Laura followed him as they made their way along the boardwalk. Pedestrians bundled against the spring chill walked up and down the water's edge. A cute little food cart sold artisanal sausage sandwiches and sodas. If she hadn't been full from lunch, she would have bought one of the delicious-smelling sandwiches.

She took a few more pictures before stopping when something across the street caught her eye. Curious, she guided Frank under another banner announcing the upcoming art fair and toward a storefront with large windows facing the street. A sandwich board proclaimed, "Welcome to the Davis Gallery, We're Open!"

A gallery, huh? Art always intrigued Laura, especially how certain artists had so much inspiration and talent.

She and Frank entered, and at once they stood inside an open, sunlit space with white walls. A carousel of art prints stood close to the reception desk, and glass shelves by the window held mouth-blown vases. Framed pictures lined the walls, most of them available for purchase. The whole space was dedicated to celebrating art.

Laura felt instantly at home.

"Can I help you?" A woman wearing a bandana over her hair stood atop a small ladder, dusting the corners of the entryway. She turned to look at Laura, who recognized her immediately—the owner of the rental house.

"Ellen!"

The older woman smiled in pleased surprise. "Laura! Hello!"

"Do you work here?" Laura asked.

"More or less." Ellen grinned. "I own the place." She climbed down from her ladder.

"This too?" Laura waved at the gallery.

"And a couple other spots in South Haven." Ellen's smile turned reflective. "My husband was a very smart investor. But he loved this gallery, so I keep it up as best I can."

Laura looked around, impressed. Everything in the space was carefully, lovingly arranged and spoke of the owner's dedication to art.

Ellen set down her duster and put an arm around Laura's shoulders. She led her toward one of the dedicated galleries. "I am so sorry about the rental situation," the older woman said. "Have you decided what you're going to do?"

Laura shrugged, though her attention was focused on the framed photographs that adorned the walls. Wow. These artists were good. Really good.

"There's nothing else available in town," she said, "so we're staying put."

"That's wonderful!" Ellen's pleasure at the fact that Laura and Spencer were stuck together seemed odd, but Laura didn't press it. Removing her arm from Laura's shoulders, Ellen adjusted a few pictures, straightening their frames so they were just right. "I'm going to return half the rental fee to both of you."

"Thank you." Laura could use that extra money to get a new lens for her camera.

"It's the least I could do." Ellen's gaze fell on the camera hanging from Laura's neck. Her eyes brightened. "You're a photographer."

Laura quickly shook her head. "Oh, no. Not at all. I just take pictures." Nobody would ever confuse her with an actual *photographer*, who created art. She was just messing around.

But Ellen looked at her intently. "You choose your frame. You choose your lens. You're a photographer." She gestured to the camera. "May I?"

"No," Laura said at once. "I never show anyone. It's just for me." The idea that an actual gallery owner like Ellen might look at her pictures made Laura want to curl up in a ball on the floor.

"None of that," Ellen said firmly. "Not in here." Her gaze fell on the partitions surrounding them.

"This is a sacred place. All art is safe within these walls."

Laura wavered. Could she finally show someone her photos? And if she did, what if Ellen laughed at them or dismissed them as amateurish and not worth looking at?

But...Ellen had said this was a place where art was safe. Maybe it was finally time to let somebody see what had been her strange preoccupation for the past fifteen years, ever since she'd been able to hold a camera on her own.

*Que será, será.*

"Okay." She unlooped the camera strap from around her neck and handed the device to Ellen. Her stomach knotted.

"Thank you." The older woman walked away as she scrolled through the photos Laura had taken that day. Laura didn't look at her pictures—all her attention was focused on Ellen's face as Laura tried to gauge her reaction.

"Mm," Ellen said. "Mm-hmm."

*What did that mean?*

"A little Adams," the older woman said softly. "Maybe some Imogen Cunningham."

In middle school, Laura had once saved up and secretly bought herself a book of famous photographers. She'd worn the pages out poring over the images. The fact that Ellen even mentioned incredible artists like Ansel Adams and Imogen Cunningham when looking at Laura's silly photos was astonishing.

"You don't photograph people?" Ellen asked.

"No," Laura exclaimed. "I'd be way too embarrassed to even try. That's too personal."

Ellen looked at her like a teacher whose student had just claimed that two plus two equaled five. "Nonsense. The human face is the greatest subject of all." She turned back to the camera, scrolling through more pictures. "You have an eye."

Laura gaped at her. "I do?"

"Mm-hmm. My husband and I made it our mission to encourage young artists. I'm trying to carry it on, but it's not so easy these days." She cocked her head. "Hey, maybe you would like to help me."

"Excuse me?" Laura couldn't have heard right.

"Here, at the gallery." Ellen looked around at the space. "There is so much you could do. Catalogue, arrange things. In return," she went on before Laura could answer, "I'll teach you everything I've learned. We could even study the great photographers together. Arbus. Cartier-Bresson." Her excitement rose. "Maybe throw in some Warhol for fun."

"Thank you," Laura said politely. Surely Ellen had to be joking. "But I'm only here for two weeks."

Instead of looking disappointed by this, the older

woman appeared even more delighted. "Absolutely perfect. The South Haven Art Fair is two weeks away. I have a big show that weekend and I could use some help."

Did Laura dare? This place was for art and people who knew about art. She was just a business major living at home, taking pictures for her own entertainment.

"Can I think about it?" she asked.

Ellen returned the camera to her. "Of course." She walked toward the exit of the photography area, then turned to fix Laura with a penetrating expression. "You have a talent, Laura. It would be a shame to let it go to waste."

With that, the older woman walked off to take care of gallery business, leaving Laura alone with Frank, her camera, and thoughts of what might be.

When Laura returned to the rental house that afternoon, she was so preoccupied with thinking about Ellen's offer that she didn't check to see if Mozart—and Spencer—were out. Moments after she and her dog got inside, Frank lunged with a bark, breaking her hold on his leash.

"No, Frank!" But it was too late. He was already

heading toward the couch where Spencer sat and Mozart perched on the back.

Yet instead of chasing the cat, Frank sat himself down on the sofa beside an amused Spencer. Mozart didn't even blink, let alone run away.

"Huh," Laura said in surprise. "I think Frank may be getting used to her."

"Good." Spencer stood and walked toward the kitchen, giving Mozart a pat along the way. "Because I've come up with a solution to our living situation."

"You have?" She thought they'd already figured it out, but okay.

"Uh-huh. Right over here." He headed toward the kitchen counter, and she followed. Spencer picked up a sheet of paper and handed it to her.

She scanned it. "'Treaty for Living Under the Same Roof,'" she read aloud.

He looked very pleased with himself. "I thought since we have to compromise, we might as well set some ground rules."

Oh, brother.

Continuing to read aloud, she said, "'Music shall only be played in the common areas between the hours of seven a.m. and nine p.m., and at a sound level of sixty decibels or less.'"

"I measured the volume on your speakers," he said. He added in a low, confiding voice, "It was eighty-eight."

She stared at him for a moment before reading. "'Pet access to the common areas will be on strict rotation, with feline activity limited to even hours and canine activity during odd hours.'"

Out of the corner of her eye, she saw Spencer silently mouthing the words that he was so clearly proud of.

"I think that is perfectly reasonable," he said. "Don't you?"

She had no answer for him, so she kept on reading. "'Residents may occupy bathroom a maximum of three times per day, with a limit of twenty minutes per usage.'"

For real? Laura remembered reading some random trivia that humans went to the bathroom at least six to seven times a day, so unless Spencer had a way to alter biology, he was going to be disappointed when neither one of them could stick to using the bathroom only three times daily.

"Oh," he said, pulling out a pen. "One more thing." He wrote on the paper. "'Two towels maximum.'"

The words Laura thought would definitely earn her a reprimand from her mother. But jeez, Spencer was crossing the line with this "treaty."

"I forgot," he added. "To make things even easier…" He walked quickly to the refrigerator and opened the door.

Laura's mouth dropped open. No. He hadn't.

But he had. A line of green tape stretched right down the middle of the fridge, dividing it. Her food had been arranged on one side, and his on the other.

"Half for you," Spencer said, "half for me."

He turned to her and beamed as if he'd just invented calorie-free ice cream. "So? What do you think?"

She opened her mouth to speak, but thought better of it. All she could do was glare at him.

Two weeks with him seemed like an eternity.

# Chapter Nine

"Frank, what are we going to do?"

Laura lay flat on her back in the middle of the bedroom floor, staring at the ceiling. Her dog sat right by her head, and his tail thumped with blissful, unconcerned doggie happiness, despite the fact that his owner was having a crisis.

She'd thought that she and Spencer were finally starting to get along, especially after talking about their families, but then he'd given her that treaty, and she'd been forced to rethink their strange relationship.

After that treaty, he'd become absolutely unbearable.

"First," she said, "Professor Perfect wakes me again with his dumb jump rope at *six in the morning*. I'm on vacation. I'm not supposed to get up at six in the morning.

"And then," she went on, more irritation in her voice, "I'm just trying to have a quiet cup of coffee. You know, trying to wake up after being deprived of sleep? So there I am, minding my own business, reading the paper, and then WHIR! Spencer the Smoothie Prince causes a racket making one of his disgusting green drinks in the blender. Can't he just have pancakes and bacon like a normal person?"

Frank panted in reply.

"Sure, I think," Laura said. "Fine. I'll just have myself a nice, relaxing hot shower. Wrong!" She groaned in exasperation. "I'm just rinsing out conditioner when the Almighty Shower Monitor bangs on the door and tells me my time is up. I don't even have five minutes to dry my hair. You know what a disaster my hair is if I don't properly dry it. Like some kind of prisoner, I have to march out of the bathroom while he just looks at me like *I've* done something wrong."

She turned her head to look at her dog, who gave a soft whine of understanding. "I don't think I can take much more of this, Frank. I swear, if he does one more thing to annoy me, then we're out the door—treaty or no treaty."

Frank edged closer to her and licked her nose.

Despite her foul mood, she giggled. Her dog always knew exactly what she needed.

"Okay." She sighed and sat up. "You're right. I

shouldn't hide in my room. Let's go out on that nice patio and just chill. He can't bother me if I'm outside."

When she got to her feet, Frank leapt to his paws. She grabbed a glossy fashion magazine and her camera, and with her dog following, she headed downstairs.

Cautiously, she poked her head into the living room. Spencer sat at the desk, staring at his computer as if he hoped it would get up and start talking. From the looks of things, he hadn't written anything. Maybe he was storing up all his genius so it could pour out of him like a shaken-up soda can.

Annoyance tugged at her when she realized she was hiding from him. She had just as much right to be in this house as he did. Tilting up her chin, she walked out into the living room and toward the doors leading to the patio, all the while conscious not to look in Spencer's direction. Frank's nails clicked on the hardwood floor as he trailed after her.

Once outside, Laura parked herself in a chair and Frank did the same. She turned on her portable radio and cranked the volume as one of her favorite songs played. Losing herself in the music, she happily perused the magazine, paying special attention to the way the images were photographed. They were primarily studio shots, but the ones that interested her the most were location pictures. Some of the photos looked like works of art, so she studied them to see how they had been composed, and the use of light and dark. Maybe if she—

*Tap tap tap!*

She looked up at the sound. It was coming from behind her, in the house.

Swiveling in her seat, she saw an annoyed-looking Spencer standing at the window behind her. He angrily pointed at her radio and gestured for her to turn it down.

*Now I can't listen to my music? Oh, heck, no.*

Purposefully ignoring him, she turned back to her magazine. He'd just have to learn to deal with a little music. Besides, it wasn't like he was churning out words.

Behind her, the door to the patio opened. She glanced up when Spencer came striding out. After sending her one irritated look, he turned down the volume on her song until it was almost inaudible. Then he strutted back inside.

Laura set her magazine down and stared at the lake, outwardly calm even though her pulse was thudding.

She marched inside, Frank following, and banged cabinets as she looked for something to have for lunch.

"Could you keep it down?" Spencer said from his desk.

"Sure," she answered before slamming the cabinet. But she didn't want to prove to him that she was some kind of petulant child, so she quietly took out a pot and filled it with water. In a few minutes, she was stirring up a serving of macaroni and cheese.

She sat down at the kitchen counter to eat her meal, and then became aware of Spencer hovering behind her.

"Seriously?" She refused to turn around to look at him. "My *lunch* is bothering you?"

"The whole house smells like powdered cheese." He came around the counter so that he faced her, bracing his hands on the countertop.

"I can't help that." She glanced at the plate of broccoli sitting next to his computer. "Some people like to eat things that are actually cooked. You know, cooking? It's one of the hallmarks of human civilization."

"Humans have also evolved to the point where they can make rational, sane decisions," he said.

"Here's my decision: I'm going to have my lunch in the media room and watch a movie while I eat." She stood and grabbed her bowl. As she strolled toward the room, Spencer trailed after her. "What now?"

"I won't be able to work if you've got the television on."

She whirled on him. "Wear headphones."

He scowled at her deliberate repeating of his earlier words to her. "I can't focus with music on."

"That is *your* problem." She walked into the media room and heaved a sigh when he appeared in the doorway. "For someone who wants nothing to do with me, you sure do like to follow me around."

"I don't think you understand how important it is that I finish this paper."

"Explain it to me."

He dragged his hands through his hair. "My *future* is on the line."

She felt a tug of sympathy. "I'm trying to get along, but you're the one who refuses to let me do anything. I paid for this place, too."

"To just hang out and do nothing. You don't take anything seriously."

Setting her bowl aside on a table, she planted her hands on her hips. "Excuse me? You know *nothing* about me."

"I know enough," he said tightly. He strode over to the television and grabbed the remote. "I'm keeping this. The television stays off until *I* say otherwise."

*I am done with this. I'm done with him. Nothing is worth putting up with Doctor Smarty Pants.*

She picked up her bowl and the very last of her patience. Coldly, she said, "You get your wish."

"What does that mean?"

"It means," she said, glaring at him, "I can't take another minute with you. Waking me up at the crack of dawn. Disturbing my peaceful morning with your death machine of a blender. Hurrying me out of the bathroom before I can even dry my darned hair. And now this?" She pointed to the remote in his hand. "If I wanted to live with my parents, I would have just stayed home."

He opened his mouth to speak, but she was finished. She went into the kitchen and threw the remains of her food into the garbage. Then she stomped up the stairs, Frank beside her, and stormed into her bedroom. She grabbed her empty suitcases and flung them onto the bed.

Frank whimpered and she felt badly for distressing her dog, but she couldn't calm down. After tugging open the dresser drawers, she collected her belongings and shoved them into her bags.

"So, you're going?" Spencer said from the doorway.

"Wow, Professor." She wadded up some shirts and rammed them into her duffel. "You're really observant."

"What about the treaty?"

"You can take that treaty and—" No. Her parents had raised her better than that. She inhaled, fighting for calm. "It doesn't matter." With all her things packed, she closed her bags and hefted them. "Come on, Frank."

Spencer stepped aside as she left the bedroom. He didn't look as triumphant about her leaving as she would've expected, but he didn't try to stop her from going, either. Like a perfectly groomed ghost, he trailed after her as she went downstairs and plopped her bags down. She pulled out her phone and used a rideshare app to call for a lift.

"Where will you go?" Spencer asked. "None of the hotels take pets."

She whirled on him. "If you're so concerned about my well-being, maybe you shouldn't act like the warden at a juvenile detention center."

"There are rules—"

"Okay. I'm done." She snapped Frank's leash on the dog's collar, then corralled her bags before walking to the front door and opening it. "Enjoy your stay, Mr. Hodkins. I hope it's productive."

She didn't wait to hear his response before slamming the door shut behind her. Hope of a dramatic exit died when she had to wait a full ten minutes for her ride to arrive. Part of her almost expected Spencer to come outside and try to convince her to stay, maybe insisting that he'd loosen up a little so they could both remain at the house. But that was another hope that didn't survive long. He stayed in the house.

Finally, as the sun was beginning to set, her ride showed up. She and the driver got her bags in the trunk and she gave him Rose's address. Frank climbed into the backseat and Laura got in after him.

She almost didn't look behind her as the car pulled away. Almost.

Kenny and Rose couldn't have been more gracious when Laura and Frank showed up at the door to their house. All Laura had to say was a forlorn, "Hi," before the Changs stepped aside to welcome her inside.

It didn't take long for Laura to bring them up to speed on the "Spencer Hodkins, Fun Killer" situation. She had to rein herself in to keep from using foul language, but every time she thought about Spencer, her temper spiked. And the most frustrating thing of all was that she'd actually started to *like* Spencer. Yet he was too stuck in his ways to make room for anyone or anything.

*Good luck to Susan*. Because there was no way Laura could endure living with Spencer.

When she calmed down a bit, Rose fixed them a simple dinner of stir-fry and Kenny poured Laura a generous glass of white wine. The meal and sauvignon blanc helped dull the edges of her temper, so that when Kenny made up the sofa into a guest bed, Laura felt exhausted.

While her husband tucked in sheets and smoothed out blankets, Rose asked, "So, this guy actually made a list of rules he expects you to follow?"

"Right down to the towels," Laura said drily.

Both Rose and Kenny shook their heads in disbelief.

It sounded even more unreasonable when Laura said everything out loud.

"Can't you just kick him out?" Kenny asked, fluffing a pillow.

"He signed the papers," Laura said. "He's got just as much right to be there as I do." It was annoying, but the truth.

Rose wrapped her arms around Laura and squeezed her tightly—at least, as tightly as her belly would allow. "You're welcome to stay here as long as you want."

"Thanks, you guys," Laura said. "For everything." She glanced at the clock and saw that it was getting pretty late. Guilt poked at her. "Now, please go to sleep. I don't want you to do anything else." When the Changs hesitated, she added, "Please, go."

Everyone said their goodnights, and then Rose and Kenny headed upstairs to their bedroom. When she was alone, Laura plopped down on the sofa. She patted the place beside her.

"Come here, Frank." He eagerly jumped up, and she rubbed his head. "This is more like it, huh?"

She looked around. Rose and Kenny didn't have a very big house—in fact, even the couch was tiny—but it was warm and comfortable and, best of all, wasn't occupied by an extremely handsome but equally uptight doctoral candidate. The situation at the Changs' wasn't ideal, but it had to be better than putting up with Spencer's inhuman regulations.

Right?

The house was quiet. Very, very quiet. It seemed much bigger now, too. Almost…too big. Too empty.

Spencer sighed in exasperation as he fixed himself a late-night snack. He chopped up carrots and arranged them neatly on a plate. This was better than having to smell all of Laura's sugary, greasy—delicious—food while he prepared his meals. He wouldn't have to face her looks of disgust when he drank his kale smoothies, and he didn't have to worry about taking up too much space in the refrigerator.

Mozart could be out whenever she wanted. In fact, right now, she lounged on the sofa. He was only imagining her looking around, searching for Frank.

The dog, and his owner, were gone. The house was Spencer's. Completely his. Exactly what he wanted.

"This is more like it, huh, Mozart?" He carried his "food" into the living room and set it on the desk. "Finally, some peace and quiet. I'm going to get a lot of work done."

He sat down and stared at his computer. The screen was almost empty.

"Lots of work," he said slowly.

He continued to look at the screen, but no words magically appeared.

The silence in the house was oppressive, both thick and empty at the same time. He didn't hear anyone upstairs, or out on the patio singing along with the radio, or playing with her dog. It was just...desolate.

Spencer glanced over at Mozart, who stared at him in that uncanny way of hers, like she was looking into his soul. "What?"

The cat didn't blink.

"It wasn't my fault." Spencer spread his hands. "It was her choice to leave. That's what she wanted. Besides," he added, "it's not a good idea to have somebody like her around when you're trying to do work. Tossing her hair all the time. Walking around the house." He paused, remembering Laura's laugh and the way they had talked about their families. And her blue eyes and pixie-like nose. "Being all cute."

Mozart seemed unswayed by his arguments.

Spencer took a bite of carrot, but it wasn't nearly as comforting as s'mores.

Lying on the sofa with the lights off, Laura wished she had her old photography book to peruse. It always made her feel better to look at the pictures, like no matter how crazy or mixed up her life was, somebody out there knew what they were doing.

But the book was held together now with duct tape on the spine, and it sat on the bookshelf in her bedroom back home.

She couldn't listen to music, either, since she didn't like headphones and she didn't want to wake Kenny and Rose. All she could do was lie there in the darkness with Frank curled up beside her, staring at the ceiling and trying not to think about Spencer.

Tomorrow was Rose's baby shower, so Laura needed to get some rest for the big day. As the best friend of the mother-to-be, she would be running around making sure everyone was fed and happy.

"Isn't this better?" she asked her dog. "Isn't it, Frank? Just you and me." The way it had been for a long time. "No one telling us to be quiet all the time. Drinking that weird stuff that he always drinks. Waking me up first thing in the morning to do his sit-ups. With his abs all…" She exhaled, remembering how good Spencer looked in the morning sunlight. "Like that."

She wouldn't think about how nice it had been when they had sat beside the fire pit, sharing s'mores and stories about themselves. How he'd really listened to her and seemed to understand what it was like to live in her parents' shadows. And how he'd been a little sad when he'd talked about his own folks and the questions he couldn't ask them. She had resisted brushing the hair off his forehead because she didn't know if he wanted to be touched, and also she had realized that touching him probably wasn't a good idea.

He had a girlfriend. A life.

And he wasn't her problem anymore. Which was how she wanted it.

*Stop thinking in circles and go to sleep,* she thought sternly.

She closed her eyes, but her body wasn't comfortable squeezed between Frank and the back of the sofa. "No, help," she said irritably. "You have to move."

Frank only stretched out and yawned.

"No," she said again, struggling to find a good position. The sofa was so tiny. "Frank. I can't—"

She wriggled, but it didn't help. Nothing helped. She flopped around like a fish and then, suddenly, there was no sofa beneath her.

Laura fell to the ground with a thud.

It was going to be a long night, and a very long two weeks.

# Chapter Ten

It turned out that spending the night on the floor while your dog slept on the nearby sofa was not a great way to sleep. Who knew?

Sunlight poked through the curtains and Laura squeezed her eyes shut, trying to block out the brightness. At best, she'd been able to get a handful of hours of sleep, but she had kept waking up and remembering with a grumble that she could have been lying in a king-sized bed in a beautiful room overlooking a lake. She could have, if it hadn't been for one Spencer Hodkins, the bane of her existence.

*Buzzzzzzz!*

"I'm up," Laura said groggily. "I'm up."

She slapped the top of the coffee table, thinking to shut off the alarm clock. But the irritating sound didn't stop. Pushing herself upright, she realized that the noise was the doorbell. It took way too much effort to pull herself upright and shuffle to the front door.

Yawning as she pulled it open, she revealed a guy standing on the front porch. Her sleep-clouded eyes registered a floppy haircut, a sweatshirt under a varsity jacket, and far too much enthusiasm for this hour of the morning.

"Hey," the guy said cheerfully.

"Hi." More conversation was beyond her.

"You must be Laura, right?"

Who was this guy, and how did he know her name? "Uh-huh."

"Cool." The guy beamed at her, and she vaguely recognized that he was cute in a *hang loose* kind of way. "I'm Tyler, friend of Kenny's. I'm here for breakfast."

He brushed past her on his way inside.

"Come on in, Tyler," Laura said under her breath. She was definitely not in the mood for chirpy surfer dudes, but it was Rose and Kenny's house, so she was just going to have to make nice.

The Changs came down in their pajamas, and Kenny and Tyler greeted each other with fist bumps and back slaps. Rose shot a glance toward Laura. *Bros.*

Laura rolled her eyes in acknowledgment. She'd had enough of men for a while. Sure, Kenny was okay, but he was the exception.

While Kenny made breakfast, Laura went into the bathroom to change. Tyler might be a friend of a friend, but that didn't mean she wanted him to see her without actual pants.

She brushed her teeth and splashed water on her face, hoping it would chase away the dark circles under her eyes. At least she wasn't being timed.

When she came downstairs, the table was already set with four places, including big glasses of orange juice and a platter full of a delicious-smelling scramble. Laura joined Rose in the kitchen as Tyler and Kenny sat at the table and talked excitedly about Tyler's latest snowboarding trip to Switzerland.

"You *have* to go to Zermatt, dude." Tyler's hair got particularly floppy when he discussed snowboarding. "They have some of the most insane verticals you have ever seen."

Kenny looked impressed. "Sounds amazing."

The two friends continued to babble about things like *shreddin' the gnar* and *pow* as Laura helped Rose pile toast onto a plate.

"Cute, isn't he?" Rose asked quietly.

Laura glanced at Tyler, who was demonstrating for Kenny how he *tore it up* in the Alps. He was good looking, if somebody liked the super sporty type. He definitely wasn't a PhD candidate. "Uh, yeah, I guess."

Rose looked at her. "You guess? Come on, Laura,

he's adorable. Maybe," she said in a sly voice, "you guys should go out sometime."

"I'm just not really interested in dating right now," Laura said.

Her friend's eyes softened. "Are you really going to let that thing with David stop you from meeting the right guy?"

It was strange, but after Laura's first day in South Haven, she hadn't thought about David at all. She'd been too preoccupied trying to share a roof with a blond psychology grad student.

"You think this is the right guy?" Laura looked back at Tyler as he laughed at something Kenny said.

"I don't know," Rose answered. "But neither will you if you don't take a chance. Whatever happened to the old Laura? *Que será, será?*" She grabbed a bowl of fruit and carried it to the table.

Her friend had a point. Picking up the plate of toast, Laura followed Rose into the dining area.

"Kenny says you've got a crazy cat guy at your house," Tyler said as she sat. He took a bite of toast before anyone else could grab a piece.

Laura's hackles rose. Yeah, she had her issues with Spencer, but she didn't like the way Tyler was talking about him. "He's not crazy," she said. "He's just sensitive."

"He doesn't like loud music," Kenny said. "He doesn't let her use the shower when she wants."

"Whoa." Tyler held up his hands. "You gotta get rid of this guy."

"It's not that easy," Laura said. "He's got a contract."

"Maybe you need to convince him to break it," Rose said.

Laura raised her eyebrows. "And how do you suggest I do that?"

Gesturing with his toast, Tyler said, "Figure out what bothers him, and then do it." He grinned. "A lot."

There was a lull as everybody considered this.

"Laura…" Rose said slowly. "How would you like to host my baby shower?"

All four of them at the table stared at each other in disbelief. Laura couldn't believe sweet Rose would ever think of something like that. The plan was outrageous, diabolical…and very promising.

The morning had been completely unproductive for Spencer. Yet again, he'd spent hours with his hands hovering above his keyboard but not actually typing. The silence in the house had started to wear on him, and he had actually hoped Mozart would knock a piece of bric-a-brac off a shelf to interrupt the quiet.

A couple of times, he'd picked up his phone

intending to text Laura and invite her back. Maybe having her around wasn't really that troublesome. Maybe…it was nice with her sharing the rental house. At the very least, she provided a distraction from his writer's block.

But then he'd remember that he didn't have her cell number, and so he never got in touch with his invitation.

Full of restless energy, Spencer paced in the living room. His whole body practically vibrated with the need to move or do *something* other than glower at his laptop. Even though he'd worked out first thing that morning, he couldn't seem to settle down.

He hurried upstairs and into his bedroom. Despite the fact that Laura had gone and he could take the larger master, he'd decided it would be too much trouble to transfer all his belongings from one dresser to the other. Besides, Laura might change her mind and want to come back. It made sense to stay where he was.

Mozart slept on the bed and didn't stir as he changed into his exercise clothes and sneakers. He didn't like the idea of her roaming around the house while he was out, so, after tucking his phone into his pocket, he left the bedroom and shut the door behind him.

Downstairs, he went to grab his jump rope and

mat. Yet when he looked outside, he saw how the lakeshore beach formed a track perfect for running. It was a little gray and misty out there, but that didn't bother him. Maybe some fresh air and mist might help him quiet his body down and get his mind focused on the dissertation.

Fortunately, the rental property had a spare set of earbuds tucked into a utility drawer. He plugged them into his phone and scanned through the streaming music channels. You couldn't really run to classical music. Same with 1940s oldies. Out of curiosity, he selected a channel playing pop music. Upbeat, peppy sounds filled his ears, and it made him smile, thinking about the way he and Laura had battled it out over her music.

His smile faded when he remembered that it was their fight over her radio that had pushed her closer to leaving. And his confiscation of the remote had been the last straw. *That* had been pretty high-handed of him.

There was no taking it back, especially since he couldn't get hold of her. Maybe Ahmed at the rental company could reach out to Laura and let her know that he'd offered to have her come back. The idea seemed like a good one. Once he finished his run, he'd contact Ahmed and see what could be done.

He stepped outside and turned up the volume on

the music. It had a good beat, so after warming up, he took off at a brisk pace.

Almost at once, he felt better. His feet dug into the soft sand and he took big breaths, deeply inhaling the fresh lakeside air. Why didn't he run outside more often? Usually, he'd get on the treadmill at the university gym and just pound mindlessly. But here in nature, there was so much to see—the glassy surface of the lake reflected the slate gray sky, and trees swayed in the breeze. A few ducks paddled in the middle of the water, while a woman in a small sailboat waved to him.

He waved back and kept going. As he did, his thoughts drifted. Maybe he was approaching his dissertation topic all wrong. Maybe his central premise needed rethinking. Was love truly just a chemical reaction, or was there something about it that defied science and learning? Certainly the pop song he was listening to seemed to find the subject of love endlessly inspiring.

The fact that he didn't know how he felt pushed him to run faster, as if to outpace his uncertainty.

Still, he couldn't stay out here forever. The day was moving on toward afternoon, and he should really get back and work. He turned around and started back toward the house.

When the house loomed up in his sights, his phone

rang. He slowed and saw on the screen that the caller was Susan. He turned off the music.

"Hey, honey," he said when he answered.

"Spencer?" Susan looked concerned. "Are you all right?"

He probably looked a bit sweaty and breathless, which wasn't how she normally got to see him. "I just went for a run."

"There's a gym in that little town?"

"No," he said. "I went for a run on the beach."

"Outside?" She sounded shocked.

"Yeah," he answered. "You should see this place! It's so beautiful." Maybe when his dissertation was finished and defended, they could celebrate by renting the house again, just the two of them.

Susan frowned. "Spencer, it sounds to me like you're not actually getting any work done."

"That is not true." He climbed the grassy slope leading to the house. "In fact, I'm right on the verge of a major breakthrough." Kind of. Possibly?

He reached the wraparound patio and headed toward the door that opened onto the dining area adjoining the kitchen and living room.

"I hope so," Susan said doubtfully.

"Don't worry. There's absolutely nothing that's going to stand in the way of me and finishing my paper."

He opened the door. And was met by a wall of women's voices.

Stepping inside, he saw that the living room was filled with pastel balloons and women in dresses. *It's a Boy!* one balloon proclaimed. A pregnant Asian woman on the sofa was opening a box and lifting up a tiny onesie. She held it up for the crowd and everyone collectively cooed.

There was a baby shower happening in his rental house.

"Susan," Spencer said, fighting for calm, "I'm going to have to call you back." He didn't wait for her response before disconnecting.

He stepped into the living room. "Excuse me," he said, waving his hand so he could get the women's attention. "Hi, excuse me."

A dozen pairs of female eyes all turned to him.

"Rose," an East Indian woman said as she looked at him flirtatiously, "you didn't tell us there was going to be entertainment."

Oh, no. He was *not* stripping down to bump-and-grind music while women waved cash at him. He might be a graduate student strapped for cash, but taking off his clothes for money wasn't in the game plan. Anyway, weren't strippers part of bachelorette parties, not baby showers? It probably wasn't a good idea to ask these hungry-eyed women.

"Oh, Spencer." Laura walked out of the kitchen. She wore a flowered dress and carried a bottle of champagne. She blinked innocently at him. "You're home early."

"Apparently." He turned to the shower guests. "Sorry to interrupt." He said to Laura in a surprisingly even voice, "May I speak with you in the kitchen, please?"

She followed him into the kitchen and had the nerve to look at him as if coming home to an empty house and finding a baby shower in full swing was something that happened every day. Yes, she looked very pretty in her dress—but that wasn't the point.

"I thought you were going to be staying with your friends," he said.

She shrugged. "It didn't really work out, so I came back."

"I can see that. And what's with all this?" He waved toward the colorful banners and balloons and decorating the house.

"It's Rose's baby shower," Laura said as if to say, *Duh*.

"Why is it happening here?"

She shrugged again. "It was the only place that could fit everybody."

Was she kidding? "And you didn't bother telling me this because…?"

"You're so busy with your paper," she said. "And I didn't want to disturb you. I know how sensitive you are," she added with completely false sincerity before leaving him alone in the kitchen.

Fine. That was how she wanted to play it. Seeing that there was no use in arguing now, especially as the shower guests seemed comfortably settled in, he sighed and strode toward the stairs. As he passed the women, several shot him frisky smiles and waved goodbye. He smiled politely. Good to know he had a career option as a stripper if he couldn't make a living in psychology research.

He took the stairs two at a time, muttering to himself. "'I just know how sensitive you are,'" he parroted. She had a lot of nerve!

Reaching his room, he opened the door.

His cat shot past him, running downstairs, straight for the baby shower.

"No, Mozart!"

But she was gone. A second later, Frank darted out of Laura's room in pursuit of Mozart.

"No," Spencer shouted. "Frank!"

It was too late. The pets were headed right into trouble.

# Chapter Eleven

Laura was just pouring a guest a glass of champagne when she heard Spencer yelling upstairs. She didn't have much time to wonder what he was so upset about before Mozart ran between the legs of the women. Frank was hot on her trail, barking excitedly as he played his game of tag.

As the animals raced past, confusion and chaos followed. One of the guests dropped her cake on her blouse, and Mrs. Woods spilled champagne across herself. Shrieks of outrage followed.

Laura immediately went into action. "Frank!" she called. "No, Frank!"

She was joined by Spencer, who ran after his cat.

They chased the animals around the room,

fruitlessly shouting their names. Mozart leapt up onto Spencer's desk.

"My notes!" Spencer yelled, but Mozart had already run across the neat stacks of cards and scattered them all over the floor.

Frank kept up his happy barking, thoroughly convinced this was a fun game. He chased Mozart as the cat slipped between the table holding Spencer's record player and the wall. Her dog immediately followed. The table wobbled dangerously.

Oh, no. Laura and Spencer lunged to stop it from falling. But they didn't reach it in time. It crashed to the floor, sending the phonograph and the record on the turntable flying. They smashed apart into fragments.

Spencer's record—the one he'd searched for over a year to find—was nothing but black shards.

The guests quieted down, and even the animals seemed to sense that something was very wrong.

Laura's horrified gaze shot to Spencer. He wore a look of resigned dismay as he stared at the destruction.

"Oops," she said.

Clearly, the party was over. The guests got to their feet and headed out. Laura held the door for them as disgruntled women in stained and messy dresses filed outside.

"Lovely party," Anisha Chandran muttered as she walked past.

"Thank you," Laura said, even though she knew Anisha was being sarcastic.

Rose brought up the rear. She shook the teddy bear she carried at Laura. "You didn't tell me he was so cute!"

"Goodbye, Rose." Laura couldn't help but chuckle. Trust Rose to find the silver lining in the situation.

Once everyone was gone, Laura shut the door and headed back to clean up the mess. Her heart sank when she found Spencer gathering up the pieces of the broken record.

"Spencer, I'm so sorry."

"That's okay," he said tonelessly. "It was just an old record anyhow." He moved to the desk and collected the scattered notecards.

"Is there anything I can do?" Laura asked.

"I think you've done enough." He snapped his laptop shut and shoved it into a case.

"I didn't mean for this to happen." She stepped forward with one beseeching hand out.

"Of course you didn't." He shook his head. "I just can't believe you'd be so disrespectful. We agreed to share this house, and now look at it." He stuffed the notecards into the computer bag.

Laura didn't want to survey the damage she and the pets had caused. "All we have to do is keep Frank and Mozart apart."

Spencer faced her. "It's not going to be a problem anymore." He gripped the bag's handle and walked toward the stairs. "Because I'm leaving and I'm taking my cat with me. Here, Mozart!"

Her stomach dropped, and she followed him as he climbed the steps, still calling for his cat.

"What?" she exclaimed. "Come on, you don't have to leave. Spencer, we can work this out." Now that she had what she had hoped for, she found she didn't want it anymore.

"Why should we? You hate planning, I hate surprises." They reached the landing and he looked at her with exasperation. "We're not a perfect match."

"But there's nothing in South Haven. We've already tried. Where are you going to go?"

"As far away from—" He stopped and looked away, and she knew what he wanted to say. But instead, he finished, "This house, as I can."

Sadness swamped her. She'd really made a mess of things, and, worse, she'd hurt Spencer. That hadn't been part of the plan.

"Mozart!" Spencer called. "Furball, come on." In search of his cat, he headed toward the bathroom.

An idea struck Laura. "I think I know where she is."

Intrigued, Spencer went with her as she went into her bedroom. He followed her lead as she got down on the floor, and side by side they both looked under the bed.

Sure enough, there were Frank and Mozart. Together. The cat seemed completely happy as the dog lay near her. It wasn't Christmas, but it sure felt like a Christmas miracle.

"I don't believe it." Spencer chuckled in disbelief.

"At least *they're* getting along," Laura said dejectedly.

After a moment, he said, "That cake really did go everywhere, huh?"

Laura couldn't stop the laugh that bubbled up as she recalled the utter madness that had followed in the pets' wake. "Poor Mrs. Woods and the champagne." And poor Rose, who would likely have all her copier privileges revoked.

Spencer laughed with her, but then they both fell silent.

"It was really quiet around here last night with you gone," he said softly.

"You must have enjoyed that."

"No, actually," he said. "I didn't."

*That* was unexpected. She could only look at him as he lay beside her.

"I know it's wrong and I shouldn't be feeling this way," he continued, "but I really missed you."

Her pulse thudded in response. And she realized something. "I missed you, too."

For several moments, they watched Mozart and Frank as the animals seemed blissfully unaware of the drama they had caused. The dog and cat almost looked like they liked each other.

"Are you really going to leave?" Laura asked.

Spencer turned to look at her, and they both realized at the same time that they were very close to each other. Close enough to kiss…

"Laura." Was it her imagination, or was he looking at her mouth?

The doorbell rang, interrupting the moment.

"I'll get it." She got to her feet and left the bedroom. *What was that?*

Downstairs, she opened the door, revealing a young guy holding a pizza box.

"There must be some sort of mistake," she said, puzzled. "I didn't order any pizza."

"I did," Spencer said as he came up behind her. He handed the delivery guy some money. "Thanks. Keep the change." He took the pizza box and closed the door.

"You," she said in disbelief as he carried the pizza into the living room, "ordered pizza? I thought you were eating raw."

He stopped and faced her. "Maybe it's time I started trying to do things a little differently." His smile was hesitant as he gestured to the box. "You want to share it with me?"

She glanced down at the logo on the pizza box, then looked back up at him. "On one condition." She gave him a wide smile. "Can we make it three towels instead of two?"

His laugh was deep and made her feel warm all over. "Okay. Three towels."

Together, they walked into the kitchen.

Maybe today wasn't such a disaster, after all.

After Spencer grabbed a quick shower and Laura changed out of her party clothes, they took the pizza—and Frank—out onto the patio so they could eat and admire the lake. She lit a fire, just in case they wanted s'mores later.

Laura hadn't seen Spencer so relaxed since…well…ever. It gave her a soft, comfy feeling to see how quickly he could smile and laugh, such a contrast from uptight Professor Perfect.

She draped herself over one of the Adirondack chairs as he turned up the volume on her radio. When upbeat music floated out, he sat down in the other chair and they both dug into the pizza. The food had gotten a little cold, but neither of them seemed to mind.

"Tell me about you and Rose," he said and then took a bite.

"We met on freshman orientation day. With her angelic smile, I thought she was going to be one of those shy, studious girls." She laughed. "Boy, was I wrong."

"Really?" He looked surprised. "She was the only one who didn't freak out because of the high-speed animal parade. I thought she'd be easy-going and mellow."

"The Rose I knew in college went a hundred miles an hour." A memory made Laura smile. "On our first night in the dorms, she dragged me and an MP3 player out to the quad so we could have a dance party. By the time the campus police broke it up, there were fifty people dancing to Rihanna."

"Should I know who that is?" Spencer asked with a frown.

She stared at him. "You don't know Rihanna?"

He gave a sheepish shrug. "Been a little busy."

"'Umbrella'? 'We Found Love'? 'Only Girl'?"

"You can keep reciting song titles, and I'm still not going to know who you're talking about."

Laura reached over to silence the radio, then pulled up a Rihanna track on her phone. "Disturbia" began playing. "I love old songs, but you've got to admit this is pretty great."

To her surprise, he didn't grimace or look appalled. Instead, after a few moments, he bobbed his head with the music. "Nice. Got a good beat."

"You're not going to call it modern nonsense?"

He shook a fist at her and said in a funny voice, "Kids today and their noise!"

She giggled, liking this unexpectedly silly side of him.

"So, Rose got you into trouble?" he asked.

"We were both troublemakers. I mean, we got our work done, and we both graduated, but it was kind of a miracle. There were many nights that we opted for karaoke instead of studying." She shot him a look. "You know what karaoke is, right?"

He pressed a hand to his chest as if offended. "I'm uncool, but even *I* know about karaoke. I don't do it, of course."

"Of course," she said with a sage nod. "But if you did, what would you sing?"

"Hm." He appeared thoughtful. "'Witchcraft' or 'The Way You Look Tonight.' My dad loved the crooners." His grin flashed. "Like Frank Sinatra."

Could he *be* any more adorable? "Good taste."

"The best." His smile faded and he seemed wistful.

Laura didn't dare ask him more than he was willing to tell, so she didn't say any more about his parents.

There seemed to be a big hurt there, and she had to respect his desire to protect himself.

After a moment, he said, "It must be strange to see Rose married and about to have a baby."

"It is." Laura sighed. "I just feel like she's gotten it together, you know? And I...haven't."

He gave her a sympathetic smile. "Remember that boat I talked about when we had s'mores? Maybe sometimes we're out sailing and we reach an island. It's a nice island, with palm trees and coconuts and lots of fish. But it's not the right island. So we get back in our boat and we go on sailing."

"You're saying I just need to keep looking?" When he nodded, she said, "Pretty wise words, Professor Hodkins."

He held up his hands. "Not a professor yet."

"Didn't mean to jinx it." She grimaced.

"I'm just being superstitious." He took another bite of pizza and chewed thoughtfully. "I haven't even written anything on my dissertation yet, let alone defended it."

Her eyes went wide. "Nothing?"

He grimly shook his head. "I keep trying, but I can't seem to get the words down."

"No wonder you've been so crabby." She winked at him so he knew she was only kidding. Partly.

"Yeah, well," he said on a grumble, "you'd be

crabby too if your academic muse was gone and your girlfriend kept reminding you how important it was that you don't mess anything up."

Talk of his girlfriend put a heavy weight in her chest. How could she forget that he was with someone? But when they were hanging out like this, really connecting, it was easy to overlook.

"Is there anything I can do to help?" she asked.

He exhaled heavily. "Thanks, but I don't think so. It's just a matter of sitting down, clearing my head, and getting it done."

"You know what helps a bad case of writer's block?"

Sitting up, he asked, "What?"

She grabbed a bag of marshmallows from the table and waggled it. "It's been scientifically proven that the combination of graham crackers, chocolate, and marshmallows helps promote creativity and intelligence."

"Perfectly roasted marshmallows," he added.

"Naturally."

Spencer finished off the last of his pizza before reaching for the marshmallow toasting sticks. "Let's test that hypothesis."

As Laura reached for the graham crackers, she had to admit that with a little pizza in him, Spencer Hodkins was one terrific guy.

# Chapter Twelve

The next day, Laura summoned her courage and went back to the Davis Gallery. She wasn't certain about making this decision, but if Spencer could try new things, maybe she could, too.

Entering the gallery, she saw Ellen showing a couple around the photography space.

"These are part of a series the photographer did in one day," Ellen said, gesturing to a series of pictures, "telling the story of a single flower from dawn until dusk." She caught sight of Laura waiting nearby and excused herself to walk over.

"Laura, it's so good to see you!" They hugged. "I hope everything is still okay at the house."

"It's amazing," Laura said. She'd gone to bed last

night smiling and hadn't even minded when Frank had snored.

"And Spencer?" Ellen asked.

"Oh no." Laura was quick to assure her. "We're loving it. But, Ellen…" She gathered up her nerve. "I just wanted to ask you—"

"Yes," Ellen said with a smile. "The offer still stands. Come back tomorrow and we'll get started."

Laura grinned and, after she and Ellen set a time for her to return, left the gallery. She had thought that after talking with Ellen, she would grab lunch on the boardwalk, but she was so excited she had to hurry back to the house to tell Spencer.

When she stepped inside, she saw him at his desk—actually typing. Her heart kicked with happiness to see him working. After last night's conversation, she'd been a little worried about him. Dissertations were a big deal, and it seemed like there was extra pressure on him to not only get his done, but excel.

Frank trotted up and she gave him a pet before waiting patiently as Spencer continued to type. Finally, Spencer looked up from his work and smiled at her.

"Looks like someone's in a good mood," he said.

"I am!" She stepped closer, passing Mozart on the sofa. While she scratched under the cat's chin, she said, "While I'm here, Ellen said I could work at the gallery. She's going to teach me all about the great photographers, too." Her grin couldn't be contained. "She asked me a few days ago, but I decided to take her up on it today. I'm pretty excited."

"That's great!" He stood up, and before either one of them knew it, they were hugging.

Both Laura and Spencer became aware of the fact that they were in each other's arms. They backed awkwardly away from each other.

He cleared his throat. "This calls for a celebration."

"Oh," she said, waving her hand dismissively, "it's totally nothing. Just a part-time job to keep me busy for the rest of the time I'm in South Haven."

He lifted a finger. "Nope. Not true. I see how much you put into taking pictures and the way you linger over art photos in magazines. This is a big deal, and we are definitely going to celebrate."

Warmth flooded through her at his enthusiasm. Even her parents were more puzzled than excited by her photography habit, but Spencer seemed to truly care.

"What do you suggest?" she asked. "Congratulatory broccoli?"

"Funny," he said wryly. "You and I are going out." He stepped over to his computer and opened up a search screen. After typing for a moment, he said, "Aha! Turns out that South Haven happens to have no fewer than two Thai restaurants, three Italian bistros, and one halal grill. Which will it be?"

"Ooh, I'd kill for some gyro." Her mouth watered just thinking about it.

He walked to a table and pocketed his keys. "Gyro it is."

"But, your work...?" She gestured to his computer.

"I can get back to it. Right now is about you and me and a skewer full of meat." He grimaced. "That sounded weird."

"It really did," she said, and they both laughed. "Don't let me forget to bring Frank something in a doggie bag." They walked toward the door. "What about Mozart?"

He looked touched that she'd think about his cat. "I learned the hard way that she's a delicate little creature."

"Like her dad?" Laura smirked.

"'Sensitive,' not 'delicate.'" He opened the front door. "Now, come on, it's time to celebrate."

Laura was so keyed up about starting at the gallery, she barely slept. Her mind kept spinning as she wondered what Ellen would have her do. Maybe she'd get to coordinate with artists, or design displays, or guide visitors around the gallery and talk about light and shadow, the way Ellen had.

She was so excited, she was already awake when Spencer started his six a.m. workout, and by the time he was done, she'd showered, carefully selected her outfit, and brewed a pot of coffee.

"Relax," he said as he blended up a smoothie. "You're going to be great."

"I hope so." She drummed her fingers on the kitchen counter.

"I know so." He poured himself a glass, then held up the pitcher. "There's extra if you want some."

She eyed the mixture dubiously. "Maybe when my stomach isn't tied in knots."

"Going to hold you to that." He took a sip and licked his lips. "Mm. Kale."

"Please." She shuddered. "I can't deal with green drinks right now."

He looked at the clock. "What time does the gallery open?"

"Ten, which means I have two hours to kill." She lowered her head to the counter and lightly thunked it against the surface. "Ugh."

"Hey, hey." He gently pulled her back from the countertop. "This is a no-head-bashing house. That's one of my rules. It's not in writing, but it's unspoken."

She groaned in pretend frustration. "Oh, fine."

Standing, she patted her thigh and her dog, snoozing nearby, picked up his head. “Let’s go for a walk, Frank. You need the relief and I need to do something besides freak out.”

Frank yelped in agreement before trotting over to her.

As she clipped the leash onto his collar, Spencer asked, “Do you need company or do you need to be alone?”

It was really considerate of him to ask instead of assume anything. “Alone,” she said. Having to keep up one end of a conversation was beyond her right now. “Hope you don’t mind.”

He smiled easily. “Not at all. Enjoy your walk. And if I don’t see you before you go to the gallery, break a leg. You’re going to be great.”

“Thanks.” Knowing that he was in her corner definitely helped her feel better.

She took Frank for a long walk as she tried to calm herself down. It was silly to be so nervous about something that had nothing to do with her career, or even anything important. But she couldn’t help being anxious.

By the time she got back to the house, Spencer had bathed and dressed and was sitting at his desk, typing away. Not wanting to disturb him, she tiptoed in and removed the leash from Frank’s collar. Her dog immediately went to Mozart on the couch, and the two animals curled up together. It was so cute Laura almost said, "Aw" aloud. But Spencer was hard at work, so she didn't say anything and crept upstairs to get her purse.

She used an app to call a ride and waited for it outside. The journey to the gallery was quick, and within minutes, she walked in the door.

"I'm so glad you're here," Ellen said, coming around the reception desk. "You can put your stuff in a drawer and then I'll give you a tour."

After securing her bag, Laura said, "I'm all set."

Ellen picked up a paint roller that Laura hadn't seen. "Great. We can start in our main exhibit area."

For the next twenty minutes, Ellen guided Laura around the gallery, pointing out where they displayed decorative arts for sale and areas that were reserved for more established artists. Laura loved all of it, especially being in the presence of so many beautiful and meaningful pieces, and the way that Ellen talked to her as if they were equals—not a woman educated in the arts and a clueless business major.

Ellen directed her into an empty space that had nothing on the walls. "This is our New Artist Gallery. Every year, I dedicate this space to a young, emerging photographer who shows real artistic promise."

*Is that so?* Laura looked around the space, trying to

imagine if she could ever be good enough to fill it with her own work.

"And you, Laura"—Ellen turned to her, and her pulse jumped. *She couldn't mean me, could she?*—"are going to paint it."

Ellen handed her the paint roller and then cheerfully walked away.

Laura had to laugh. After all the anxiety she'd felt, learning that all she had to do was get a coat of paint on the walls was pretty ridiculous. That's what she got for psyching herself out.

Wait until she told Spencer.

The next morning, Spencer was just tying the laces of his sneakers as he sat on the edge of his neatly made bed when Laura appeared in the door of his bedroom—wearing exercise clothes. She gave him a tiny uncertain smile.

He looked at the clock on his bedside table. It read 5:55.

"I'm tying my shoelaces too loudly?" he asked. "Is that why you're up?" She hadn't mentioned anything last night about needing to get up early.

"I heard that if you exercised early in the morning," Laura said, "you've got more energy through the day.

Ellen's got me working pretty hard, and I figured rather than down a vat of coffee in the afternoon, I should give this a try." She said all this lightly, as if it didn't matter what he believed, but he could see the hesitation in her eyes, like she cared what he thought.

Maybe they were rubbing off on each other.

In the short time that he'd known Laura, he had seen that she responded better to an outright challenge than to hand-holding. He stood and walked to her. "Think you can keep up?"

Her smile widened. "You're the old man graduate student. I'm more worried about *you*."

"Let's go, then." He clapped his hands together before brushing past her. This was going to be fun.

They trotted down the stairs together. He handed her the jump rope. "You start. Five minutes, no breaks."

As she tested the rope, she looked at him. "So you're just going to watch me sweat my butt off? I don't think so." She pointed a finger at him. "Jumping jacks. Five minutes."

He grinned, caught up in the spirit of the challenge. "And if the other person stops first—"

"Dinner's on them." She stuck out her hand. "Deal."

"Deal." He wrapped his hand around hers to shake, and he jolted at the feel of his skin against hers. Something warm and alive expanded in his belly.

He mentally shook himself. It wasn't like they were giving each other back massages every night—of course it might feel weird to touch her.

Except it didn't feel weird. It felt nice. Very, very nice.

Laura also frowned at their joined hands, as if she was experiencing the same strange sensations. After a moment, she released her grip on him and they backed away from each other.

"Uh." He held up his wristwatch. "I'll time us."

"Good idea."

He pressed a button on the watch. "Go."

During the next five minutes, he could see her fighting to keep going. She did all right at the beginning, but he saw how she grimaced as she moved.

"How…much…longer?" she gasped.

Without missing a beat, he looked at his watch. "Thirty seconds."

He saw how she rallied herself, pushing her strength to its limits. Either she was really determined not to buy him dinner, or she had a lot more persistence and determination than she gave herself credit for.

"And that's time."

She dropped her arms and the jump rope fell from her hands. "Thank goodness."

"It's a draw." He looked at her with admiration. "Didn't know you had it in you."

"Never underestimate me, Mr. Hodkins," she said loftily, then smiled. "Thanks for giving me an excuse to push myself."

"You rose to the occasion. A lot of people would give up."

"That *used* to be me." She looked thoughtful. "But since I've been in South Haven, things have been... different. Maybe...*I'm* different in little ways. I mean," she added, "if you can be persuaded to eat pizza, who knows what I can do?"

It was strange to think that they were influencing one another, rubbing off on each other. Strange—but also good.

"How are you at sit-ups?"

"Not sure. I'm really good at Boat Pose in yoga."

He unrolled the exercise mat. "Up for another challenge?"

She grinned impishly. "Bring it on."

"You take the mat. I'll use the floor."

"It's your mat," she protested.

He settled the argument by lying down on the floor. When he waved toward the mat, she sighed but stretched out on it.

"Five minutes of sit-ups. Same rules. Dinner's on whoever stops first."

Instead of shaking his hand, she nodded, which

disappointed him a little. "Got it. Set that timer and we'll go."

He started the stopwatch. "Start."

As they did crunches, Frank trotted between them, completely unconcerned that he might be bothering anybody. Spencer once thought Frank's owner was just as oblivious, but he didn't think so anymore.

His ab muscles were just starting to complain when he checked the time and saw that the five minutes were up. "That's it." He propped himself up on his elbow as he faced her. "We're never going to get dinner if we keep having ties. I know," he said as an idea came to him. "You write my dissertation and *I'll* take pictures, and then we see who was the most successful."

"Hah!" She lay flat on the mat, looking up at the ceiling. "First of all, there's *no way* I could write one word about psychology. Not everybody's got a big, wrinkly brain like yours."

"And what's your second objection?"

"Anybody can take better pictures than me."

He scowled. "Don't say that. I bet your photography is really good."

"How would you know? You haven't seen it."

"Because I know you," he said. He poked a finger into her shoulder. "I see the way you study your subject matter before taking a picture, and how you're composing a shot." He shook his head. "I think you're too hard on yourself. Maybe it's time to recognize that you're a lot more special than you realize."

She blinked at him, and he realized he'd said a lot. Perhaps too much. But darn it, it made him angry when she put herself down. He truly did hope she saw how extraordinary she was.

"Mister Hodkins," she said. "You say that now, but what will you feel when…"

He braced himself for her telling him to mind his own business.

"…I beat you at sprints on the beach."

Oh. Okay. A corner of his mouth curled into a smile. "Same rules?"

"Same rules."

They got to their feet at the same time and raced out the back door, laughing all the while.

In the end, they had to split the cost of dinner.

# Chapter Thirteen

"Do you have a few minutes?" Ellen asked.

Laura looked up from the computer. She blinked to refocus her eyes on the older woman who had come into the gallery's back office. The first coat of paint in the New Artist Gallery was drying, so she'd been assigned the task of cataloguing the artists and works for the upcoming arts festival.

Good thing she'd exercised with Spencer today. Otherwise she'd nod off doing the repetitive work. Thinking of how he'd not only challenged her but encouraged her made her smile. She'd left him that morning as he'd pounded away at his keyboard.

"Of course," she said.

Ellen stepped out of the office and waved for Laura

to follow. "Bring your tablet." When Laura caught up with her, Ellen was in a main gallery room.

"Do these need to be catalogued, too?" Laura asked, holding her tablet in the crook of her arm.

"They're already in our database. I hoped you and I could spend a little time looking at some photographs. Maybe broaden your horizons." Ellen smiled. She looked at the digital device Laura carried. "That's for taking notes. You up for some Photography 101?"

"That would be great!" Laura had been looking more seriously on her phone at fine art photography, trying to pick each picture apart, but it would be much better to have someone with real experience and knowledge guide her.

"Tell me what you see here." The older woman gestured toward a black-and-white photograph of a stairwell in some European country.

"Movement." Laura studied the picture. "Everything points the viewer upward as if they're rising higher and higher. The shadows make it look almost sinister, but the big diagonal block of light interrupts that feeling. It's like there may be darkness, but then there's also hope." She looked at Ellen and wrinkled her nose. "I'm totally babbling."

Ellen laughed. "You aren't! You're making perfect sense." She nodded approvingly. "And you have great instincts. You know how to read a photograph."

"I do?" Laura asked in disbelief.

"You do." She pointed at the picture. "There's something in photography called *the rule of thirds.* Have you heard about it?" When Laura shook her head, Ellen continued. "You divide the frame into three parts—horizontally and vertically. It's like overlaying a grid of nine squares over each image. The lines of the grid intersect at different points. When you take a photograph, you put your points of interest in the intersections. You can also place subjects along the lines of the grid."

"Sounds mathematical," Laura said. She wasn't afraid of numbers since she used them every day at her job.

"It is, in a way. But after a while it becomes instinctive." Over the photo on the wall, Ellen drew an invisible grid with her finger. "You see here how parts of this picture line up with the intersections and how things are balanced on the grid. Nothing's perfectly symmetrical. That gives it rhythm."

Laura slowly nodded. "So, if you use the rule of thirds, it gives each image visual harmony."

"Exactly! The person viewing the picture is drawn in. They *want* to interact with the photograph." Ellen's smile was wide. "I knew you would get this."

Her praise made a bubble of happiness rise up in Laura. She opened a document on her tablet and quickly typed up what she and Ellen had just discussed. "Can I see more?"

"Sure." Ellen led her to a color photograph of dunes in the desert. "Shooting in color requires different skills. But you prefer black and white, don't you? I bet that's because you like old films."

"How did you…?" Then Laura realized Ellen had seen her rental questionnaire, which had included her favorite film, *Casablanca*. "I guess you're right. I never thought about what drew me to taking pictures in black and white."

"It makes your subject matter automatically more dramatic."

"It does," Laura said. "And it's more romantic."

The corners of Ellen's eyes crinkled. "So you *are* a romantic."

Was she? Even though she watched modern movies, she kept going back again and again to classics, where people found each other and overcame incredible obstacles on their way to love. If only her life was like one of those movies. But most of those films featured smart, driven women who knew what they wanted to do with their lives—and men who loved them for being smart and driven.

"Maybe I am." Laura glanced at the picture of the dunes. "Can we look at more black-and-white stuff?"

Ellen walked to a picture of a lot that was vacant

except for a shed in the process of falling down. "This is one of the first pieces that I bought. Do you see how the light is hitting the shed?"

"It's amazing." Laura stepped closer to take it in.

"Because the photographer took the picture at dawn. Light is always better at dawn and dusk. So instead of sleeping in or going to happy hour, it benefits an artist to go out and be in the world. *That's* when you get the best shots."

Laura jotted that down on her tablet. She was going to have to exercise some discipline to make use of Ellen's advice, but it might make her own photos better.

The older woman went on. "Even though this photograph is of a subject that people might not consider beautiful, the true artist can find meaning and inspiration in anything. Don't be afraid to go where your eye and instinct take you. Trust yourself."

The phone rang and when Laura took a step to answer it, Ellen held up a hand. "I'll get it. You keep looking at the photographs, and think about what I said." She hurried toward the reception desk.

Alone, Laura stood in front of the picture of the vacant lot. Ellen's words echoed through her, making her think about what made her choose certain subjects over others, and how she positioned something within the frame.

*Trust yourself.* Could she? Laura was so used to doubting what she wanted, but maybe it was possible to ignore that doubt and let her feelings guide her.

She smiled to herself. She sounded like a Jedi—but maybe people responded to the Force because it made sense and took away fear.

Look at Spencer. He couldn't write when he had gotten to South Haven, but something had changed in him, allowing him to work. Perhaps he was also learning how to trust himself.

*If he can do it, so can I.*

By the time Spencer got downstairs for his six a.m. workout, not only was Laura already dressed, but she looked like she'd been out already. She came inside from the back patio, holding her camera.

"How long have you been up?" he asked with surprise.

"Since five." But she didn't look tired. Instead, her cheeks were pink—either from excitement or the cool dawn air—and she looked absolutely adorable. "I was taking pictures. Ellen told me that the best shots are at dawn and dusk, so I wanted to see for myself."

"And?"

She beamed. "It was *amazing*. I saw so much

wildlife. And the *light,* Spencer." She bounced charmingly. "It was so beautiful."

"Can I?" He pointed at her camera, hoping to get a look.

To his disappointment, she clutched the camera to her chest. "I'm not ready yet."

"I'm going to hold you to that *yet.* It means that there will come a time in the future when I will get to see your pictures."

"Only if I get to read your paper," she fired back.

"Having trouble sleeping? Because I'm certain it will bore you into unconsciousness." He was only half joking. The dissertation was taking shape, but he wasn't certain if it was any good.

She set her camera down and stalked over to him. "Nope. No way, Mr. Hodkins. So long as we're both under this roof, neither one of us is allowed to say mean things about ourselves."

He looked at her as she had a take-no-prisoners look on her face. It was like being ordered around by a pixie, but he didn't mind. "That's one of *your* rules?"

"Sure is. Along with 's'mores and pizza are both essential food groups.'"

"Noted." He held up his jump rope. "Ready for today's challenge?"

She planted her hands on her hips like a superhero. "I was born ready."

"Give me *ten minutes* of jump rope."

Even though she groaned, she took the exercise equipment from him. "That means ten minutes of jumping jacks for you."

"All right." He didn't give away any uncertainty, even though he'd never tried to do ten solid minutes of jumping jacks before.

Laura asked, "What do I get when you lose?"

"Oh ho! *When*, not *if*. Getting cocky, Ms. Haley."

"Got to think positively," she said wisely.

"Because you're a positive person." It seemed like so long ago when they had first collided in the house, and it also felt like only a few minutes had passed.

She looked at him meaningfully. "So, what do I get?"

"Four towels instead of three. And what do I get when *you* lose?"

Her finger tapped against her chin as she thought about it. "I'll clean the leftover goop from your blender."

Washing out the blender was always irritating. "I accept your terms."

"Ready?" He held up his wristwatch.

"As one tomato said to the other, 'Ketchup.'"

He frowned for a moment, and then her joke caught up to him. Now it was his turn to groan. "Promise me you'll never make another pun."

"I won't...*if* you beat me."

Spencer felt his mouth curve into a grin. She had a way of making him smile. He didn't know how it happened, but whenever he was with her, he grinned like a kid set loose in the model airplane aisle at the toy store.

"Three, two, one," he said. "Go!"

Later in the day, Laura walked to the gallery. As she ambled through town, she hummed to herself, unable to tamp down the bubbly feeling she'd had all morning. Yet her fizzy mood didn't stop her from stopping to take pictures along her way to work.

The light wasn't as perfect as it had been at dawn, but she still shot. Remembering what Ellen had said about the rule of thirds, she carefully arranged each image.

She snapped a photo of a statue. It was as close to taking a portrait as she was comfortable getting. At least this subject was made of bronze, so she wasn't getting too personal. Looking in the viewfinder on her camera, she studied the picture.

*I'm getting close, but I'm not there yet.*

Checking the time on her phone, she gulped as she realized she was five minutes late. She hurried to the gallery as fast as she could without attracting too much notice.

"I'm so sorry," she gasped to Ellen as she rushed through the front door. "I got caught up taking photos."

The older woman gave her a stern look. "You've made a commitment here, Laura. I expect you to honor it."

Laura felt her face heat. "It won't happen again."

"Dedicated artists are disciplined."

After putting her camera away in a drawer behind the reception desk, Laura ducked her head. "Got it."

"Good." Ellen held up a folder containing sheaves of paper. "I'm going to need you to review these release forms and check them against the list of artists participating in the upcoming show. Contact anyone who hasn't sent in their release form."

"Sure." Laura took the folder and thumbed through it. The project might take a while, but she felt eager to get to it.

"Oh, one other thing," Ellen added. She nodded toward a stack of books piled at one end of the reception desk. "Those are from my collection. There's Ansel Adams, LaToya Ruby Frazier, Imogen Cunningham, and Masumi Hayashi, just for starters."

"Do you want me to shelve them?" Laura asked.

"No, dear," Ellen said gently. "I want you to *study*

them. Take as long as you like." With that, she strolled away into an adjoining gallery.

For a moment, Laura only stared at the books. Then she gathered them up in her arms, as if they were something precious. Because they were.

# Chapter Fourteen

Another morning, another smoothie. Spencer grabbed kale, spinach, and an apple from the fridge and prepped everything to go into the blender.

He didn't mind it so much, especially now that his month of eating raw had turned into a month of occasionally eating pizza and Thai food. He figured that if Susan ever asked about his diet, he could tell her without lying too much that it was going well.

He winced at the thought of last night's phone call with his girlfriend. Spencer always timed it to coincide with Laura's evening walk with Frank. When Susan had asked about whether or not he was lonely being by himself in the house with just Mozart for company, he'd only said that he was getting a lot of work done. That was true, at least.

Laura entered the kitchen, showered and dressed after their morning workout. After giving the blender a whirr, he poured out two glasses of green liquid.

Without speaking, he handed the second glass to Laura. "You always say you'll try it tomorrow," he said. "Tomorrow is today."

She glanced at the smoothie, wearing a comical look of doubt. But instead of offering him more excuses, she shrugged and took a sip.

He waited for her to spit it out or at least make a face. Instead, she appeared reluctantly pleased. "Not bad." She drank a little more. "I mean, it's not pancakes and bacon, but I think I can work with this." After they clinked their glasses together, she strolled out of the kitchen and didn't see Spencer grin.

A meow at his feet caught his attention. He looked down to see Mozart staring at him judgmentally.

*Have you forgotten someone?* Mozart's expression seemed to say.

"What?" Spencer asked.

The cat sauntered off, her tail in the air.

He sighed, not knowing how to feel. Guilt ate at him, and yet he looked forward each morning to the exercise competition he and Laura would have, and he anticipated her coming home in the evenings so they could talk about their days.

Even grocery shopping with her had become

interesting. Yesterday, they had both brought lists with them, a big change from her grabbing packages of instant ramen and boxed macaroni and cheese at random. She'd been so adorably proud of her list, too, showing it to him with an air of accomplishment.

When he'd leaned closer so he could see it, they had both realized at the same time that they had been standing close. Very close. The air between them had become charged—right there in the produce aisle.

It was getting harder and harder to remind himself that he couldn't, shouldn't kiss her. But, boy, did he want to.

"I'm taking off," she said, entering the kitchen with her empty glass.

"The gallery doesn't open for a few hours."

After rinsing out her glass, she held up her camera, which hung from her neck. "The light's so good this morning, I thought I'd take some pictures before going in to the gallery."

He leaned against the counter, enjoying the way her face lit up whenever she talked about her photography. It was a far cry from the uncertainty she'd shown the first day they'd met. "Been shooting a lot. It's nice."

She blushed prettily. "I think I may be getting it. The more photos I take, the more I'm learning."

"Think you'll keep it up when you go back home?" he asked.

"I can't think that far ahead." Her gaze slid away, and a slightly oppressive silence fell, as if neither of them wanted to consider life after South Haven. After a minute, she said, "Time to go. I'll see you tonight."

"Sure. It'll be me and Frank and Mozart waiting for you. Just us animals."

"Hah! Like you're a wild animal." With that, she sailed out the door.

"You've got no idea," he muttered to himself.

When he'd finished his smoothie and had showered and dressed, he approached his desk. It hadn't been that long ago that sitting down here to work had felt like approaching the executioner's block, but that had changed.

Sitting down, he stretched out his fingers before he began to type. Thoughts and ideas flowed out of him, and though he didn't quite agree with his thesis statement anymore, he kept going. It was too late to find a new topic, so he needed to stick with this one.

The next time he looked up, it was already lunch. He fixed himself a salad and ate it quickly. Tonight, he planned on making a vegetable lasagna, so he needed to keep everything light up until then. Once lunch was finished, it was back to work.

Evening was already starting to fall by the time he wrapped up for the day. Laura had been taking pictures on her way home, so he took Frank on a walk.

Although Spencer hadn't considered himself a dog person, he had to admit there was something fun about the way Frank approached the world with so much excitement and enthusiasm. Between trotting happily down the street, the dog eagerly sniffed everything. Almost nothing escaped his notice. All the while, he panted merrily and his tail never stopped wagging.

"There's something to be said for being a dog, isn't there, Frank?" Spencer asked as the dog nosed at the edge of a flowerbed in front of a house. While Frank continued to poke around, Spencer observed how the flowers were a colorful assortment of pinks and purples. If the dog hadn't made him stop, most likely Spencer wouldn't have noticed the blooms. He should tell Laura about this house and its pretty flowers. She might like to take a picture of it.

When he let himself in at the rental house, Laura's voice sang out from the kitchen. "I picked up some celery on my way home. It looked like you were running low."

"Thanks," Spencer said, touched by her thoughtfulness. He walked into the kitchen with Frank and found her chopping up celery.

The dog jogged to his owner and placed his paws on her knees. "Hey, Frank! Were you giving Spencer a hard time today?" She set down her knife and ruffled his ears.

"He and Mozart slept on the sofa all day. Eating salad for lunch means no dogs beg for a bite of your food. Speaking of which, how about I make us some vegetable lasagna for dinner?"

She brightened, then looked at him suspiciously. "Are you going to use eggplant instead of noodles?"

He laughed. "Even *I* have my limits."

"In that case, I approve of the lasagna plan. How can I help?"

He pulled a can of tomatoes from the pantry. "I could use a sous chef."

She gave him a smart salute. "Reporting for duty."

As they prepared their meal, she chatted about the visitors to the gallery that day, including a man and his husband who had bought the most expensive photograph in the gallery. "It would be so amazing to be able to just buy art whenever I wanted it."

"You can make your own." He dropped the noodles into a pot of boiling water.

She tilted her head to one side. "Huh. Maybe I could. Hey," she said, her eyes going wide, "I haven't asked you how work went for you today."

He shrugged. "More boring neurochemical stuff."

"No talking badly about ourselves, remember?" She pointed a carrot at him.

"Right, right." He sighed as he took the carrot from her and started to chop it up. "I'm just wondering if I'm going down the correct path with my paper."

She looked at him with concern. "What can you do if it doesn't seem right? Can you start over?"

"There's no time. I have to submit it to my professors in a week."

Shaking her head, she stirred the pot of tomato sauce. "Wow—I can't believe we've been here so long."

"Me either. It's like—"

"No time has passed," they said in unison.

For a second, they stared at each other. Now they were finishing each other's sentences. Things were getting very…interesting.

As they sat down to dinner later, Laura said, "I've got an idea. Want to go to the movies after we eat?"

"I can go one better," he said as he filled her wineglass. "The media room has a ton of classic films. Why don't you pick one out and we can watch it here?"

"Ooh, I like it! I think there's popcorn in the pantry. Do you trust my taste in movies?"

"If you like *Casablanca*, I trust you."

"I've narrowed down our selections," Laura said as Spencer settled down in his chair in the media room. Mozart jumped into his lap while Laura held up two DVD cases. "I'm in an Audrey Hepburn mood. *Breakfast at Tiffany's* or *Roman Holiday*? I do have to warn you, though, that I ugly cry whenever I watch *Roman Holiday*."

"*Breakfast at Tiffany's*," he said at once.

She slid the DVD into the player. "Can't handle a woman's tears?"

"I don't want to see you cry." He pressed play on the remote.

"That's the nicest thing anybody's ever said to me," she said as she dropped into her chair. As Frank settled at her feet, she picked up the bowl of popcorn and held it out to Spencer.

He took a handful of popcorn. "Maybe you ought to set your bar higher."

"Maybe." The opening credits started. "Another warning, I talk back to movies."

"That's got to be awkward when you go to the movie theater." He chewed on some popcorn.

"I have to eat the whole time to keep myself from blabbing over the film. Oh, I love this movie," she said on a sigh as Audrey Hepburn looked in the windows at Tiffany's.

She wasn't wrong about talking back to the movie. "Don't say that to her, you idiot!" or "I'd *kill* for that dress," or "Don't trust that guy!"

It didn't annoy Spencer at all. In fact, he found it kind of cute. She threw herself into the experience of watching a film with a wholehearted enthusiasm.

And when Holly Golightly and Paul Varjak looked for Holly's cat in the rain-soaked alley, Laura grabbed Spencer's arm and gripped it tightly, her eyes fastened on the screen.

"It's going to be okay," he said with a smile.

"I know, but this scene gets me every time." A single tear rolled down her cheek as Holly found Cat and hugged the animal close. She brushed it away quickly. "Sorry."

"Don't apologize," he said, even though her tear made his chest squeeze.

The film ended with a swell of music, and Laura wiped at her eyes. "Wow. That was amazing."

But something from the movie stuck with him. "Do you think people belong to each other?"

She propped her chin in her hand. "The first few times I watched that film, I totally identified with Holly. I thought I was a wild thing, too, and didn't want to be in a cage."

"Sounds like you've changed your mind."

"Maybe Paul is right," she said thoughtfully after a moment. "Maybe the more you run, the more you're trapped by yourself."

Spencer pondered this, considering all the things in his life he ran from, and the things he ran *to*. But in every direction, all he found were his own fears. If he stopped running, where would that leave him? He didn't know, and that uncertainty scared him a little.

One thing was for certain, watching the movie with Laura had been one of the most enjoyable experiences he'd had in a while. He didn't want it to end. "Double feature? We could throw on *Casablanca*."

She yawned. "I'd love to, but I'm completely wiped out." She got to her feet and Frank did the same, shaking himself out. "Have a good night."

"You, too." When she left, heading upstairs, he petted his cat. "What do you say, Moz? Another movie?"

Mozart stretched and jumped down to the floor. She padded to the door, then looked back at him with an expression that read, *Don't you have to get up early tomorrow?*

"Fair point." He needed to remember what was important, and what he needed to put aside for his own good.

Getting to bed on the earlier side seemed to have been the right choice. Laura was full of energy during their jog on the lakeshore, talking eagerly about the work of famous photographers. Frank ran with them along the sand, as peppy as his owner.

"It's impossible to overstate the importance of early landscape photography pioneers, like Muybridge," she said animatedly as they ran. "Without him, there'd be no Adams. But Ansel Adams started with the feeling he was trying to convey, and then chose subjects which—" She broke off abruptly. "I'm babbling, aren't I?"

"No!" he answered at once. "I just love hearing you get so excited about something. You ever thought about doing it professionally?"

She turned to jog backwards. "Are you kidding? My parents would never speak to me again—ack!" She tripped over the soft sand and started to fall. He reached out to stop her.

Tumbling, they tangled up together, and in an instant, he lay on top of her on the ground.

They'd never been this close, and awareness flooded him. She went still beneath him, and they breathed the same air, their lips just inches apart.

*Don't do it,* Spencer warned himself. *Don't kiss her!*

Frank sniffed at them before loping ahead.

"Sorry about that," Spencer murmured.

Her eyes were wide. "Oops."

He had to get up or else he'd do something he'd really regret. After pushing up to standing, he helped Laura to her feet. All he could manage was an awkward smile as he jogged away, putting much-needed distance between them.

For a guy who always tried to follow the rules, he was in a lot of trouble.

# Chapter Fifteen

It seemed like no sooner had Laura painted one gallery than it was time to paint another. She'd walked in the door that morning and Ellen had handed her another can of paint and a brush, pointing her in the direction of the walls that needed attention.

Laura wanted to do a good job at whatever the older woman asked her to do, but as she ran her brush up and down the wall, she found herself drifting, thinking back to what had happened on the beach yesterday morning.

She could have sworn that Spencer had wanted to kiss her. And the crazy thing was that she'd wanted him to. More and more, she'd been wondering what it would be like if she had someone like him in her life, someone who encouraged her and made her laugh.

Someone with his own interests but who appreciated what excited her.

Someone *like* Spencer, but not *him*. That was impossible. He had a girlfriend, and Laura needed to remember that. She couldn't break up a relationship. That would make her a terrible person, so she had to remember that Spencer was just a friend, and that was how things between them were going to stay. Much as she wanted it to be different.

"It's not going to paint itself," Ellen said, breaking Laura's train of thought.

Laura smiled ruefully as the older woman walked off.

*Focus on what you* can *do. Not what you can't have.*

She had to remind herself of this later when she went out onto the back patio of the house to take pictures. Letting her lens drift from one subject to the other, she landed on Spencer standing near the water. He held a stack of note cards and reviewed them thoughtfully.

As if sensing her camera trained on him, he looked up. A little smile played about his lips. Even though she gazed through her camera at him, her stomach gave a leap. Her finger pressed down on the button before she knew what she was doing, capturing his image.

He glanced back down at his notes, and Laura reviewed the picture through her viewfinder. There still was something deeply personal about taking someone's picture, but it had just felt right to snap Spencer at an unguarded moment.

The next day, Laura cautiously approached Ellen. "I've been doing a lot of shooting. I guess you inspired me."

"That's wonderful, Laura! I'd love to see what you've done."

Laura connected a USB cable between her camera and Ellen's laptop perched atop the counter of the reception desk. She stood back, watching nervously as Ellen scrolled through her pictures.

The older woman moved fairly quickly through the shots, though she lingered longer on some more than others. But when Ellen got to the picture of Spencer, she stopped scrolling and stared at the image for a long time. She even put on her glasses.

Oh, gosh, was it really awful?

"It's your first portrait," Ellen said. She looked between Laura and the photograph. "It's good. It's very good."

Laura thought she might collapse to the floor. She smiled instead as her heart pounded. She'd done it! Taken her first portrait, and a trained expert had admired it!

This definitely called for a celebration.

The gallery was closed on Tuesdays, so that day Laura had time to take Frank on a long walk through town. She brought her camera with her, of course, but her attention was fixed on the shop displays as she and Frank strolled.

Something in a thrift store window caught her eye, and with a mischievous smile, she hurried into the shop. As she made her purchase, her belly got fluttery and nervous. She hoped she was making a good choice.

Fortunately, Spencer was in the kitchen when she came home that night with her purchase. "Stay in there," she called to him after unclipping Frank's leash. "I brought you a surprise."

"What is it?" he yelled back.

"You know what the definition of *surprise* is! Don't come out!"

"Fine, but I'm dying of curiosity in here!"

She hurriedly set up her surprise, then skipped into the kitchen, where Spencer waited impatiently. "All set. I'm going to cover your eyes and lead you out."

"Is that necessary? I can just close my eyes."

"Hey." She poked a finger into his chest. "This is my show. So you'd better do what I say."

He held up his hands. "As you wish."

Wasn't that a line from a movie in the '80s? She stepped behind him and had to get up on her tiptoes to get her hands over his eyes. "Can you see?"

"Not a thing."

"Let's go." She gently guided him from the kitchen into the living room but couldn't stop giggling anxiously. Oh, golly, she hoped he liked it. "No peeking, okay? Step, step." Finally, they reached the living room. "Open your eyes."

She lifted her hands away, giving him a look at her present.

To her delight, he actually gasped. A vintage turntable waited for him atop the table that had held his old record player.

"What?" He sounded like a kid at his birthday party. "Where did you...how did you..." He shook his head in amazement.

"Do you like it?" She couldn't keep the nervousness from her voice.

"Are you kidding?" He gazed back and forth between the turntable and her. "I love it." Before she knew what was happening, he'd wrapped her in his arms and hugged her tightly.

She breathed into the sensation of being held by him. It felt...amazing.

"Thank you," he murmured into her hair.

To her disappointment, he pulled away a moment later. "I've got to try it right now."

"Try it," she said, hoping that her pulse would calm down soon.

He went to a side table, where a stack of albums sat. After perusing them, he grabbed one sleeve and pulled out the record. Laura took the sleeve from him when he placed the LP on the turntable.

"This is perfect," he said excitedly. "I can't believe you got me another record player." He gently set down the needle, and a second later, a smooth old-time ballad began to play. The singer crooned about the wonder of being in love.

"You hear that?" Spencer asked. "You don't just hear the music. You can hear their heartbeats."

She looked at him for a long time. For someone who professed to believe in cold chemical reactions, he was a closet romantic. There was a lot about Spencer that was kept secret, but when he revealed who he truly was, she liked him more and more.

*I'm in hot water.*

He held out a hand to her. It took her a moment to realize what he intended.

"Spencer…" This was not a good idea.

"Yes," he insisted.

How could she deny him? How could she deny herself?

She slid her hands into his. He led her outside, and as the music floated over them and across the lake, he held her close while they swayed in the dance.

It should have felt awkward, or at least wrong, but dancing with Spencer was exactly the opposite. It was natural and effortless and so very nice.

Laughing, he dipped her, and she felt giddy. If she had the power to stop time, she'd do it right then, so that she and Spencer could dance together in the moonlight, and nothing had to change.

Spencer knew what he was doing wasn't right—but he couldn't seem to stop himself. It just felt so good to dance with Laura and laugh with her, so different from what his life was like back home. He'd always tried to be good and dutiful and responsible. It was what his grandparents had required of him, and how he'd dealt with his parents' long absences.

*If I'm perfect, then no one will leave.*

That was a kid's idea of logic. He'd grown up a long time ago, and yet he still clung to the notion that if he crossed his *t*'s and dotted his *i*'s, the world wouldn't fall apart. Study hard, find a woman with similar goals as his, get funding, get a job, get tenure.

It was like one of those flowcharts he'd see in reports. *If this, then this, followed by this.*

The thought of hurting anyone, especially Susan, was a sharp sting deep within him. Yet the more he considered what she desired from a romantic partner, the more he believed he wasn't the man she wanted him to be. Maybe once he had been, but now—after his time here in South Haven with Laura?

He didn't know anything anymore, and that uncertainty sat coldly at the bottom of his stomach, in contrast to the warmth he felt at being this close to Laura. She'd been generous and sweet to give him a record player. The gift had been unexpected, and all the more important because he had long ago forgiven her for the loss of his original turntable.

As they swayed together to the music, he looked down at her, and the urge to kiss her was so strong, he felt dizzy.

If he was smart, he'd pack up his stuff, his cat, and his hang-ups and go home. He was close to finishing his dissertation. Surely he could complete it back in Chicago. And if he was home, he couldn't hurt anyone. Not Laura, not Susan, and not himself.

But he didn't want to leave. He wanted to stay right where he was.

Something chirped close by. Laura jumped back before sending him a sheepish smile. "My phone."

Pulling her phone from the back pocket of her jeans, she read the screen. "It's Rose. Do you mind if I answer it? She's close to her due date and I just want to make sure everything is going okay."

"Of course," he said at once.

She pressed the button and turned slightly away. "Hey, Rose. Is something wrong? Oh, that's good. You had me worried for a second." She gave Spencer the thumbs-up sign, and he relaxed slightly. "So what's up?" A pause. "Really? Um, I think that's fine. Let me ask."

Laura covered the phone with one hand. "Rose is inviting us to karaoke."

Spencer frowned. "*Both* of us?"

"That's what she said. I mean," she said hastily, "if you don't want to do it, that's completely all right with me."

A night out with Rose meant less time for Spencer and Laura to be alone together, which, given the way he'd been thinking about Laura lately, was a good idea.

"No, I want to," he said. "But isn't South Haven a little small for a karaoke bar?"

Laura repeated the question to Rose. After a pause, Laura said, "There's one in the next town over. They'll pick us up on the way."

"It's a date," Spencer said, then immediately regretted his phrasing. "Not a *date* date. Just a few friends going to do something together. Socially. As friends." He pressed his lips together to keep from babbling more nonsense.

Laura shot him a curious glance before saying to Rose, "We're in. Just honk when you get here. Okay. Bye." She ended the call and looked at him brightly. "I think it's time for a costume change."

"You look fine." In fact, he thought she looked especially pretty in her top and jeans, but he didn't want to say that out loud.

She waved her hand. "Oh, no. The way Rose and I do karaoke, we go for the full experience. Good thing I packed a few extra outfits." She walked to the patio doors but turned back before going inside. "Are you sure you're all right with this? We can easily cancel."

"Nope," he said with a shake of his head. "You're here to spend time with Rose, right? And I've never done karaoke before. Everyone's happy."

She seemed satisfied with his answer, so with a smile, she sailed inside. Alone on the patio, Spencer rubbed at his forehead as his nerves tightened. What if he made a fool of himself? What if Laura saw him on stage and realized he was just a boring graduate student with no life? What if her friends didn't like him?

He walked quickly inside and poured himself a glass of wine. He had a feeling he was going to need it.

Laura shifted in her chair, adjusting the hem of her sequined miniskirt. Her hand moved to smooth down her black bobbed wig, and her fingers brushed her giant rhinestone earrings. She shot a look at Rose, sitting across the small table.

"You could have warned me that you weren't dressing up," Laura muttered.

"I forgot that you liked to dress up for karaoke." Rose swirled the club soda in her glass, but didn't appear at all sorry.

"We *both* liked to dress up." Laura sent an exasperated look at Spencer, who was doing a very bad job of hiding his grin. "She'd wear this pink wig, glitter eye makeup, and a tutu."

"Ah, yes," Kenny said with a fond smile, "the pink wig."

Rose gave her husband a playful swat. "I had to throw it out when one of your snowboarding buddies got maple syrup on it." She held up a hand when Laura opened her mouth. "Do. Not. Ask. Besides, that tutu won't fit around this." She patted her big belly.

Glancing around the small bar, Laura felt very self-conscious since she was the only one in the room wearing something flamboyant. Most of the others looked like bar regulars in the clothes they'd worn to work. "I am *not* getting on stage."

The stage in question was the size of a large desk, and a blue spotlight shined down on whoever was brave enough to take the microphone. A small monitor perched on a barstool, where the lyrics for songs would be displayed. The man running the karaoke machine was a tall African-American man in round mirrored sunglasses and a fringed jacket, as if the Summer of Love hadn't happened nearly fifty years ago.

"You'd better get on stage," Spencer said before taking a sip of his beer. "We made a promise on the way here, remember? If I go, you go."

Laura heaved a sigh, but really, she was eager to see him in action. She was certain he'd pick something old-fashioned, like the record he'd played earlier, and had an inkling that his singing voice was going to be endearingly off-key.

"Fine," she answered. "You first." She nodded at the stage, where a middle-aged woman finished up singing "Hungry Like the Wolf."

Kenny and Rose hooted their encouragement. "Go, Spencer!"

It was dimly lit in the bar, but she could tell that he blushed. Slowly, he rose to his feet and ambled to the man running the karaoke machine, who handed Spencer a thick binder full of songs to choose from.

After he thumbed through the selections, he pointed to one. The karaoke guy nodded and waved Spencer toward the now empty stage.

Spencer looked nervous as he climbed onto the stage and held the microphone. He steadfastly refused to make eye contact, even when Rose, Kenny, and Laura applauded.

The music began. The tune was "Fly Me to the Moon," and Spencer snapped his fingers in time with the beat.

Strangely, Laura felt nervous for him, her mouth going dry. Then he began to sing, his voice a smooth baritone, and she thought she was going to need smelling salts.

"He's good!" Kenny said as he leaned across the table.

His wife's eyes were wide as she watched Spencer croon his way through the song. "He could do this professionally."

Laura had no words as Spencer smoothly made his way through the song. It was like being back in the 1950s, hearing Sinatra in a jazz club in New York. The major difference was that Spencer wouldn't look at the audience, but she found that little quirk oddly charming.

Finally, he belted out the last notes. Only when the entire bar leapt to its feet and clapped and shouted its approval did Spencer glance up. When he did, he looked only at Laura.

Her heart jumped straight into her throat.

When the applause died down, and after Spencer accepted a high five from the karaoke guy, he made his way back to the table, smiling shyly.

"Oh my goodness, Spencer!" Laura stared at him. "Why didn't you say anything?"

"About what?" He sipped his beer.

"Don't be coy! You're an *amazing* singer."

A corner of his mouth turned up. "My grandma loves Sinatra and all the old crooners. I used to sing for her at birthdays and Christmas."

Rose wagged a finger at him. "Buttoned-down graduate student, my eye. You've been holding out on us."

He shrugged, like it was no big deal, but she could see that he liked hearing the applause and praise. "Now that I've gone, it's time for you to honor your end of our agreement." He looked at the stage meaningfully.

"I think I have a sore throat." She pressed a hand to her neck and made her eyes big and sad.

"No way," Kenny said and laughed. "A deal's a deal, Loony Laura."

"Oh, fine." She slapped her hands on the table and stood. After making her selection from the binder, she got onto the stage and took the microphone.

Unexpected nervousness fluttered in her belly. Too bad she hadn't finished her margarita before agreeing to do this.

But when she looked at Spencer, who beamed at her and nodded in encouragement, her anxiety quieted. The opening notes of "The Girl from Ipanema" floated out over the crowd, and Rose whistled approvingly.

Laura knew she wasn't a great singer, but she always had fun, and so she happily sang, letting her enthusiasm make up for her lack of talent. She was actually a little disappointed when the song finally ended. When the crowd clapped—Spencer the loudest of all—she bowed.

She made her way back to the table, and Spencer plucked a carnation out of its vase to hand it to her. Heat crept into her cheeks as she accepted the flower.

"Good choice," Kenny said as he patted her on the back.

"That was incredible," Spencer said when she took her seat.

She drank the last of her margarita before saying, "Thanks! I dedicate that song to my old roommate, Rose. Who is now getting on stage, by the way," she added.

Rose didn't protest, but she made a face as she hauled herself up to standing—aided by her husband. She sang "Born to Run," her hand cradling her stomach the whole time, and when that was over, Kenny joined her for a duet of "A Whole New World."

The evening flew by as everyone took turns at the microphone. Even Spencer went up again—enchanting her once more with his crooning ability. Truly, this was a night of surprises. He even looked at the audience for a second while he sang.

By the time midnight rolled around, Laura felt herself floating on an amazing mood. She barely remembered that she was the only one in an outrageous outfit, until her wig started itching and she took it off before plopping it onto Kenny's head.

At last, Rose pleaded exhaustion, and they left the karaoke bar with promises to the guy running the machine that they would be back.

On the car ride home, the excited energy that had kept Laura going all night finally wore out. She found herself nodding off but couldn't quite sleep because it was uncomfortable to lean her head against the passenger-side window.

"Come on," Spencer said, patting his shoulder, "I make a good pillow."

"I'm fine," she protested, her words slurring from tiredness.

"I can see that." He offered her his shoulder again. "I promise I won't put a picture of you sleeping on social media."

"You win." She edged closer and laid her head on his shoulder. It was warm and firm beneath her cheek. When he curved an arm around her shoulder to support her, she sighed, and before she knew it, she'd fallen asleep.

The next thing she became aware of was Spencer gently shaking her. "We're home," he said softly.

She blinked sleepily, then started when she realized she'd wrapped herself around him, hugging him like he was a giant teddy bear. "Sorry."

"No need to apologize," he said, but she was already undoing her seat belt and opening the car door.

"Thanks, Rose! Thanks, Kenny!" Not waiting for an answer, she waved at the Changs as she sprinted toward the front door. Embarrassment made her fumble for her keys. Oh heck—she'd been *draped* over Spencer. She probably smelled like him now.

"I've got it," he said from behind her. His key was already in his hand and she stepped aside, face burning, as he unlocked the door. The second it swung open, she raced past him and up the stairs.

"Good night," she called over her shoulder.

If he answered her, she didn't hear. She was too busy sprinting up the steps and running to hide in her room. When she shut the door to her bedroom, she leaned against it and shut her eyes.

If she wasn't committed to helping Ellen at the

gallery, she would seriously consider leaving South Haven early. Maybe it wasn't the bravest thing to do, but things with Spencer were starting to reach a point of no return, and if she didn't take action, she'd do something she would seriously regret.

# Chapter Sixteen

The next afternoon, Spencer stared at the screen of his computer in disbelief.

"That's it, Moz," he said to his cat on the nearby sofa. Frank lay beside her, peacefully napping. "It's done. I finally finished it."

Naturally, Mozart had nothing to say about the completion of his dissertation. She yawned and put her head down on Frank's side.

All Spencer had to do was print up his paper, and then get it to the professors on his defense committee. And afterward he had to tell somebody about his monumental achievement. Maybe it wasn't the greatest dissertation in the history of psychology, but it was done, and that was good enough for him.

He put the dissertation onto a thumb drive and

drove to the town's copy shop, where he printed it up. The copy shop clerk handed him a thick manila envelope.

"Good luck, man," the clerk said, holding his fist out to be bumped.

Never having fist-bumped before, Spencer did it cautiously. "Thanks." He hurried out of the copy shop and, because it was such a beautiful, sunny day, he walked the rest of the way to the gallery.

He had to tell Laura. Things between them this morning had been a little strained and strange, but even so, he knew she needed to hear the news about his paper.

When he walked into the gallery and didn't see her at the reception desk, he took a few steps and called her name. "Laura? Hello?"

"She went to the café for lunch," Ellen said. He hadn't noticed her behind the desk, but he smiled at her when she approached him. "She's been working very hard this morning. She deserved it."

"Oh, well, great!" He moved toward the door. "Thanks."

Ellen's voice stopped him. "I hope that everything's okay at the house."

"Yeah," he said without hesitation. "Everything is great."

She put a hand on his sleeve. "I really am sorry about the mix-up with the bookings."

He couldn't stop himself from smiling. "Are you kidding? This has been one of the best things that has ever happened to me." Impulsively, he leaned down and pressed a kiss on her cheek, and then he hurried outside.

The café that he remembered Laura discussing was just across from the water. It looked like a nice place, and now that he was finished with his dissertation, he could spend the remainder of his time here in South Haven taking more leisurely lunches besides quick salads at home. Maybe he could meet Laura here on her breaks.

He strode through the patio and peered in the front window. Sure enough, she sat alone at the bar, reading a photography magazine. Another spontaneous smile curled his mouth when he looked at her. She'd done so much for him.

Spencer stepped inside and walked up to her. "Hey."

Surprised, she looked up from her magazine. If she was still concerned about the odd vibe between them, she didn't show it. "Hi!"

"I'm not bothering you, am I?"

"No, of course not." She set her magazine aside and frowned with concern. "What's wrong?"

"Nothing. Everything is very right." When she gazed at him blankly, he announced, "I'm done. 'The Chemistry of Love' is complete." He brandished the manila envelope and set it on the bar.

"What?" Her face lit up. "Spencer, that's fantastic! Congratulations!"

Her happiness for him made him even more elated. "Thank you. I couldn't have gotten here without your help."

She waved a hand. "You're just being nice."

"Well," he said with a grin, "you *are* going to be paying for the champagne, so—"

"Hey! Laura, right?" Spencer turned to see a young sporty guy coming in from outside. The newcomer waved at Laura like she knew him. A tiny flare of jealousy lit in Spencer, even though he knew he had no right to feel that way.

"Hey," she answered without a lot of enthusiasm.

The newcomer looked at her expectantly. "We're sitting on the patio and I thought it was you. Remember me—Tyler? Friend of Kenny and Rose." He held out a fist for Spencer to bump. Guess it was a day for fist bumps. When Spencer slowly held out his own fist, Tyler enthusiastically knocked it. "Tyler."

"Spencer. Nice to meet—"

"So," Tyler said to Laura, "did you finally get rid of that cat guy?"

Spencer's smile froze in place. "The cat guy?"

"Remember, you were going to do the baby shower thing?" Tyler said, totally oblivious.

Something cold and hard settled in Spencer's stomach. All the happiness he'd felt a moment ago dissolved. The bite of betrayal cut him deeply. A part of him shouted that he should have known all along, but he hadn't wanted to believe anything so cynical and mean-spirited.

Laura looked stricken as she tried to meet Spencer's gaze. When he wouldn't, she said to Tyler, "It was great seeing you, Tyler."

"Maybe we can get a drink sometime." After winking at Laura, he gave a lopsided grin to Spencer. "Nice to meet you, Sandy." He bounced out the door.

Still trying to grab Spencer's attention, Laura said imploringly, "It's not even…I promise you, Spencer, it's…"

He didn't want to hear it. Grabbing his dissertation, he stormed out the door, trying to tune out Laura as she called out to him and asked him to wait.

He walked quickly down the stairs that led from the street to the boardwalk and pier. Behind him, he could hear Laura's footsteps. "Wait!" she cried.

"The baby shower was a setup." His heart pounded and his face felt hot. Her deception stung, especially after the amazing week they'd shared. "You did it deliberately to mess with me. Why?"

"Because—"

"Because you wanted me out."

"No!" She caught up with him and darted in his path. "I thought you hated me."

He drew up short, stunned. "Hated you?" She gazed up at him, regret in her eyes, and he said, "No. I don't hate you. I never did." His anger drained away. He realized at that moment that all his happiest times here in South Haven had been with her. He'd eagerly awaited her coming home from the gallery every night so they could share details of their days. And when she'd fallen asleep on him during the car ride home from karaoke, he'd been enveloped in the need to hold her closely, to protect and cherish her.

*I never even saw it happening. But it did.*

He exhaled as this realization struck him. "It was just something that I told myself."

Her gaze turned mystified. "Why?"

"So I wouldn't do this." Before he could stop himself, he closed the distance between them, cupped the back of her head, and kissed her.

She tasted sweet and soft, and when she kissed him back, he thought his heart would shoot right out of his chest.

But too soon, she pulled back. Her eyes brimmed with regret. "Spencer, we shouldn't…"

Guilt immediately washed over him. This wasn't right for many reasons, even though it had felt perfect. "I'm sorry." He stepped back. "I'm so sorry."

As fast as he could, he walked away. It was like his mistakes chased him. Despite being a careful, conscientious guy, he'd gone and messed everything up. If only Laura could forgive him, because he certainly couldn't forgive himself.

Evening's chill had set in by the time Laura got home from the gallery. She stood in the driveway for a long time, debating whether or not to go inside. Finally, she took a deep breath and went into the house.

Frank immediately bounded over to her, tail wagging.

"Hi, Frank," she said with false cheer, as if her dog might have his feelings hurt by her dour mood. "Brought you a treat." She held up a plush duck and then threw it. Frank immediately ran after the toy. Ah, to find joy in something so simple.

She drifted farther into the darkened house and saw that a record silently spun on the turntable, the needle having reached the end of the LP. It was the same album Spencer had played last night when she'd given him the turntable, the night they had danced together under the stars and she'd fallen asleep wrapped around him—when she'd given him her heart.

She saw that now. Despite all her intentions, she'd fallen hard for Spencer. And when he'd kissed her...her heart had soared high above the clouds... and crashed back down to earth as she realized that anything between them was impossible.

Much as she dreaded it, she needed to talk with him.

"Spencer? You home?" She took the needle off the record and waited for a response.

Glancing around, she spotted the blazing outdoor fire pit. Spencer sat alone on the patio.

She straightened her shoulders and headed outside, grabbing a throw blanket along the way. When she stepped onto the patio, she saw that Spencer attempted to roast marshmallows over the fire, but wasn't having much success.

Slowly, she approached. "It's cold out here. Want a blanket or something?"

"Yeah, thanks." He took it from her and set it aside before making a sound of wry frustration. He held up his stick, the marshmallow black on one side and completely untouched on the other. "You make this look a lot easier than it is. I can't even get the marshmallow to stay on the stick."

"It comes with practice. Here." She took the stick from him and nudged the marshmallow farther down so it was more secure. "I still can't believe you never did this as a kid."

"I told you, my parents didn't exactly do things by the book." He smiled sadly. "I guess that's why I'm the way that I am."

Softly, she said, "It's not so bad. The way you are."

His smile turned from sad to warm with a faraway look in his eyes. "My mom and dad, they traveled a lot. For work. They were in the Peace Corps." He sighed. "I didn't get to see them that often, but they were always laughing and smiling and having all kinds of fun." He chuckled.

"They must enjoy their lives," Laura said quietly.

"They really did," he answered. The corners of his mouth turned down. "When I was about twelve, my mom got pretty sick. It all happened pretty fast, and then..." He gazed skyward. "She was gone."

Sorrow pierced Laura's chest. How awful for a child to lose his mother. She couldn't even imagine what it would have been like if her mother was gone forever. "I'm sorry."

But Spencer didn't seem to hear her. He was off in memories, reliving the pain of his past. "It was like someone turned off a light inside my dad. I just watched him fade away over the years. And then…" He swallowed. "He was gone, too."

"Spencer," Laura whispered, aching on his behalf. How could he endure the pain of losing both his parents?

"The doctors, they said he had a weak heart." Spencer frowned, still angry at those doctors. "I just think that it was broken."

It made so much sense now. Everything about him fell into place. Her gaze landed on the manila envelope on a nearby table. She picked it up.

"Is that why you did this? 'The Chemistry of Love?'"

His lips twisted in an ironic smile. "I just thought if I could find some rational, biological reason behind the feelings of love and loss…"

"It might not happen again," Laura said. She wanted to reach out to him, to touch him and let him know that he wasn't alone, but she feared what that touch might lead to.

"Yeah." He dipped his head. "And then…I met you." His gaze found hers. "And then, for the first time I realized that it's not just a series of chemical reactions. It's something so much more." His eyes were brilliant blue and he looked at her like she was something special and precious. "And it's real."

Tears swam in Laura's eyes and choked in her throat. She was pinned between elation and misery, hearing exactly what she wanted to, but knowing that it was hopeless.

The marshmallow on her stick fell into the fire, causing sparks to fly up in little curlicues.

"Great," she muttered. "Just great."

He bent to pick up the bag at his feet. "There's more marshmallows."

"It's not about the marshmallows, Spencer." She bit back on her frustration with herself and with the world. "I don't like commitment, okay? Whenever somebody gets too serious, I take a hike." David had just been one of many guys that had come into her life, and one of many to leave. Because of her. "You know why?"

"Why?" Spencer asked softly.

"My parents." Her voice was rough with tears that wanted to fall.

"They're divorced."

She looked at him with disbelief. "Are you kidding? They've been married for thirty years."

His brow furrowed in confusion. "I'm sorry, I don't think I understand."

"Do you realize the pressure that puts on me?" She pressed a hand to her chest and felt the frantic thud of her heart.

"I get it." He nodded with understanding. "You don't want to become your parents."

How could she explain this to him? The words struggled to form. "It's not that I don't want to become them. It's that I don't think that I can *live up* to them." She pressed her lips together to keep from sobbing. "I'm afraid to even try." Lifting her gaze to his, she whispered, "Until you."

There. She'd said it. And the world didn't end—but it sure felt like it should.

Spencer spread his hands. "Laura—"

"You have a commitment," she said. Her throat was tight and aching as her eyes burned. "You have a girlfriend. And I won't be the person to come between you and Susan."

She dropped the stick and got to her feet. If she didn't get out of here soon, she'd be sobbing all over Spencer's sweater, and she wanted to preserve a little of her tattered pride.

"I won't." She turned away. "Good night."

Without waiting for him to answer, she bolted inside. She ran all the way up the stairs and, after shutting the door to her bedroom, flung herself onto her bed, where Frank and his new toy waited for her.

Finally, the tears she'd held back flowed. They wracked her body as she tried to comfort herself by petting her dog.

"Do you want a piece of advice, Frank?" He nuzzled her hand. "Never fall in love with someone who has a girlfriend."

Frank whimpered softly, snuggling closer. Thank goodness for her dog, because without him, she would go through life all alone.

The rental contract specified that Spencer still had several days left at the house. But he knew that it would just be too painful for both him and Laura if he stayed.

He trudged up to his room and pulled out his luggage, setting one case on the bed. In true cat fashion, Mozart jumped into the open suitcase. She watched him using that steady, disappointed look as he packed.

"What?" Spencer demanded. When his cat just kept looking at him, he said with frustration, "Fine. I made a mistake. I admitted it, okay? Are you just going to sit there judging me all night?"

She didn't blink.

"What if I get you tuna?" Spencer asked.

The cat reached out with her paw and tapped his hand, as if excited by the prospect of a late-night snack.

He chuckled to himself, trying to find a little relief

in laughter. But he didn't feel much like laughing, or doing anything. He wanted to knock on Laura's door and, ridiculously, ask her for advice as to how to handle the situation. Instead, he stared at his open suitcase and wondered how he'd done everything he normally tried to avoid.

It didn't matter how much theorizing he did about the neurochemical nature of love—it still hurt when you cared about someone and couldn't be with them.

He'd also hurt Susan. Hopefully, she'd never know about Laura, but even so, maybe it was time to reevaluate their relationship. If neither of them was happy, truly happy, it seemed better to go their separate ways. She deserved someone who could give her his undivided affection—someone better than Spencer.

His phone rang. Looking at the screen, he saw it was Susan. They needed to have a serious conversation, but he didn't want to do it over the phone. Already, he hadn't called her in several days. As soon as he got back to Chicago, though, they were going to sit down and discuss things. It might mean that he'd never get funding from her father, but Spencer wasn't so callous that he'd stay in a relationship with someone just to advance his career.

Heart heavy, he declined the call.

"Okay," he said to Mozart, "now you can judge me."

The cat got up, stretched, then pressed her nose into his hand as she purred. Lucky cat—her needs were simple, and easy to meet. But when it came to understanding what he wanted, things got a lot more complicated.

It was one of the longest nights of Spencer's life. He lay in bed, staring at the ceiling, a sick dread in his stomach because he knew that tomorrow would be his last day in this house. His last day with Laura. But he had to go, for everyone's sake.

Sometime shortly before dawn, he dozed off, Mozart curled up by his feet. When his alarm went off at seven, startling him awake, he slapped it off and then rubbed his face as he tried to come to consciousness.

After he'd showered and dressed, he lingered outside Laura's door. Usually she was up by now so they could work out together. But she hadn't come out. He debated whether or not to knock, then decided it would be better to let her sleep. She'd been rightfully upset last night—and he wasn't certain exactly what he could say to her that might make any of this mess better.

He went downstairs to find Mozart and Frank together on the living room sofa. Seeing how well the two pets were getting along made Spencer's chest hurt all the more. They were just animals and had no idea how their humans had complicated something that should have been easy. Mozart had been an only pet all of her life, and it was going to hurt to watch her missing Frank's companionship.

It was going to hurt not having Laura's companionship, too.

On autopilot, Spencer made himself a smoothie, leaving enough in the blender for Laura, if she wanted it. Right now, he craved the comfort of a stack of pancakes slathered in butter and syrup. But he only had the ingredients for his usual breakfast. He poured himself a glass and took it out on the patio.

For a long time, he stared at the water. He was going to miss this place and its spectacular view. He'd miss running on the shore with Laura as they egged each other on. Most of all, he'd miss spending time with her and the way she embraced life.

Saying goodbye to her was going to be awful. Yet it had to be done.

Maybe it would go easier if he practiced. That way, he'd have an idea what he was going to say, and wouldn't fumble his way through a jumble of words and poorly articulated emotions.

"Goodbye," he said. That sounded so flat. He tried again, "Good*bye*. *Good*bye." Darn, nothing sounded right. Taking a breath, he gave it another go. "Goodbyes are hard. Goodbyes are not easy. I don't like saying goodbyes." He shook his head in disgust. This wasn't going well.

"But I want you to know that I will always remember our time together here at this house." That was a little better. "I just want you to know that you changed my life." Did that even begin to touch what he was feeling? "I want you to know that I don't want to say goodbye."

"To who, Spencer?"

He whirled around to see Susan coming around the side of the house, wheeling a suitcase behind her. It felt like all the blood in his body rushed to his head as the ground beneath him wobbled unsteadily.

Susan looked at him with a puzzled expression, but that barely matched the confusion he felt in seeing her *here*.

"Susan?" He set down his glass and went quickly to her, barely managing to keep his feet beneath him. "Susan!"

"I rang," she said, "but no one answered. Who are you talking to?"

"Nobody," he answered hastily as the gears in his mind spun. "Myself. I was just working on my presentation."

Belatedly, he realized he hadn't kissed or hugged

her in greeting. But when they did kiss, it was fast and dutiful, not passionate. A moment later, she stepped back and smiled at him.

"So good to see you." He glanced into the house, praying he wouldn't see Laura come downstairs. That was the last thing anyone needed. "What are you doing here?"

"I called you last night," Susan said. "Didn't you get my message?"

Guilt perched on his shoulder like a vulture. "I must have been sleeping. I'm sorry."

She looked confused by this but said, "That explains why you weren't at the train station. I hadn't heard from you in two days. I was starting to worry that something was wrong. So I thought I'd come and see how things were going."

"Everything's great." How could he get Susan out of here before she saw Laura? And what would he do if the two women met? Cold sweat slid down his back. He thought of one thing that might distract her. "I finished it."

Susan made a quiet scream of delight and bounced on her feet, genuinely thrilled—which only made him feel like an even bigger jerk. "That's amazing! Congratulations, Spencer."

She hugged him and he was enveloped in her light floral perfume.

"Now we can spend some time together here," she continued. "This place is really lovely." Grabbing her suitcase, she headed into the house.

*Danger! Panic!*

"Where are you going?" Spencer asked nervously as he stepped forward.

"I was going to look around. Is that okay?"

"Of course," he said with strained cheer. "Of course it is. It's just a bit of a mess in there."

"I'm sure I've seen worse." She gave him a droll look before stepping inside.

Spencer darted ahead of her, glancing anxiously around the kitchen and living room. Maybe Laura would stay in her room and he could get Susan out of here without anyone being the wiser. Maybe…

"Wow, Spencer." Susan glanced around, taking in the relaxed lakeside cottage decor. "I'm surprised you like this place. It's not really you at all."

Edging further into the living room, Spencer grimaced in surprise when he spotted Frank on the sofa.

"Stay," he whispered to the dog.

"Hm?" Susan asked from the kitchen.

"Stay in here and just relax," Spencer said ad lib. "I'm going to go get Mozart. She missed you a lot."

Before Susan could answer, Spencer darted away and hurried upstairs. He glanced into Laura's room, but it was empty save for her unmade bed. *Not good.*

"Spencer," Susan called from downstairs. "She's down here."

He ignored her and stood in front of the closed bathroom door. The sounds of a hair dryer whirred inside the bathroom. "Laura!" Spencer tried to speak as quietly as possible but still have Laura hear him. "Stay in there. Do not come out."

Susan marched up the stairs, wearing a very puzzled look. "Spencer. There's a dog in the house."

*No. No.*

"Yes," he said with a sunny smile. "The dog…"

"What's it doing in here?" Susan's confusion was giving way to annoyance. "Whose is it?"

*Think of something. Don't just gape at her.*

The hair dryer stopped and the bathroom door opened. "All yours," Laura announced as she appeared in a robe. She stopped short when she saw Susan, who glared at her.

His stomach dropped to his feet. He thought, half with fear and half with hope, that the ceiling would collapse.

The worst had happened.

"It's a funny story, really," Spencer said faintly. "It…"

Susan turned on her heel and stormed downstairs. Spencer exchanged a look with Laura before charging after his girlfriend.

"Who is she?" Susan demanded as she stood in the

middle of the living room, her arms crossed over her chest. "Is that her dog? Is she the old guy with the smelly mutt?"

"I'm sorry," he said at once.

Laura appeared behind him, but she was still in her bathrobe—which didn't help his case. "There was a mix-up with the rental company," she said. "They double-booked the house and no place nearby took pets."

Susan did not appear at all comforted by this explanation. She refused to look at Laura and scowled at Spencer.

"I should have been honest with you," he said, taking a step toward her.

"That's the first true thing you've said to me in a long time."

"Well," he said with a sheepish smile, "I was telling you the truth when I said I finished my dissertation."

She gave him a look that screamed, *Really?*

"Okay." He held up his hands. "I messed up. Really messed up. But I knew you'd be upset—"

"This is *my* fault?"

"Maybe I should leave you guys alone," Laura said quietly. "It was really nice meeting you," she said to Susan.

His girlfriend's mouth formed a thin line. "Yeah. It's been great."

Spencer shot Laura a glance full of apology, but

she was already climbing the stairs. He turned back to Susan. "I'm sorry. From the beginning, I screwed up. I don't have a good explanation. I just hope that, at some point in the future, you won't hate me."

"I want to leave," Susan said icily. "There's a train back to Chicago at ten. Are you going to be on it with me?"

He had to make everything right. He had to undo the damage he'd caused. "I'll be there."

# Chapter Seventeen

By the time Laura had dressed and gone downstairs, Susan already sat in the passenger seat of Spencer's rental car, waiting for him.

Laura's chest felt weighted with lead as she saw Spencer load his luggage into the vehicle's trunk. In the foyer, Mozart crouched inside her carrier and Frank sat on the other side of the grate, whining softly as he looked at the cat.

*I know how you feel, buddy.*

Laura stood with her dog, watching Spencer put the last bag—Susan's bag—in the trunk. He murmured something to his girlfriend before drifting over to where Laura stood.

"I'm so sorry, Spencer," she said. "I tried to explain the mix-up and—"

"It's my fault." He looked like a man on one of those old-fashioned torture racks. "I should have told her from the beginning."

"Why didn't you?"

He stared at her for a long time. "I don't know. I guess I probably didn't want to admit it to myself." He exhaled in a jagged rush. "It's been a very interesting two weeks."

They both nodded at that.

He offered her his hand, and they shook stiffly, like strangers. "I'll never forget…you."

Laura couldn't speak. Not without crying. So she gazed at him with regret and love and all the feelings she could never express with words.

After one last lingering look, Spencer wrapped his hand around the handle of Mozart's carrier and moved it to the car. Susan's gaze was fixed on her lap, her hair covering her face, but Laura could feel the disappointment and sadness coming from her like invisible waves.

Unable to watch Spencer drive away and out of her life, Laura closed the door and headed toward the kitchen.

"Come on, Frank."

She stopped at her dog's low, distressed noise. Turning back, she saw him at the window in the foyer. If animals felt longing and loss, surely Frank felt it now as he stared at the car pulling away.

Laura stood next to him. "Say goodbye, Frank." She fought to keep her lower lip from trembling.

All too soon, the car was gone, and so was Spencer. She drifted away from the window, intending to get herself some breakfast, but she stopped when she saw that he'd left his record player behind. A folded index card bearing her name sat atop the turntable. She opened the card.

*Please take care of this for me*, he'd written.

She dashed her hand across her eyes, pushing back the tears. She could manage this. It hurt now, but she'd survive. Somehow.

Though she wasn't hungry, she still had a full day at the gallery and needed to eat something before heading out for work. She pulled a pizza box out of the fridge, but the two cold slices inside looked unappetizing—and unhealthy.

Spencer had left her a glass of smoothie, but it had settled and separated, so after giving the blender a rinse, she prepared herself a fresh drink. As she walked from the kitchen with her breakfast, she spotted Frank lying on the sofa in the same spot he'd shared with Mozart.

Her phone rang with a call from Ellen. Despite not wanting to talk to anybody, Laura answered it. "Hey, Ellen."

"What's wrong?"

"Nothing," Laura said. "It's fine."

"I can hear it in your voice. Something's upset you."

Laura swallowed around more tears. "Spencer left today."

"But he had a few more days there!"

"His girlfriend showed up," Laura said flatly.

"Oh." Ellen sounded almost as disappointed as Laura felt. "If you don't want to come in today, that's okay."

"No, I want to come in. It'll keep me busy." Laura sipped at her smoothie, but Spencer had a way of making it taste better than a bunch of pureed vegetables. She put her drink on the coffee table and sat down beside Frank. She laid her hand on his flank. "I'm good. Really. I have Frank to keep me company."

"Bring him with you today," Ellen said.

"Are you sure?" Laura stroked his smooth coat, and his tail thumped listlessly. "He's actually kind of depressed that the cat's gone."

"That settles it," Ellen said. "Come in with Frank. And take your time. Bring your camera so you can do some shooting. The best art comes from a broken heart."

"Who said anyone's heart was broken?" Laura hadn't told Ellen about her feelings for Spencer, or the kiss.

"My mistake," the older woman said. "You just

sound like a woman carrying a lot of sadness." The sound of typing came through the phone. "Like I said, take your time getting here. I can hold down the fort for a while."

"Thanks, Ellen," Laura said.

"I'm sorry it worked out this way." Ellen disconnected and Laura stared at her phone for a moment. The gallery owner was insightful, and she seemed to know exactly what Laura needed.

After dumping out her smoothie, Laura collected her things, including her dog and her camera. A long walk would definitely help, and who knew, maybe Ellen was right and Laura could channel her sadness into her art.

Because perhaps it *was* art. Not just random photographs that she took for herself, but a point of view she expressed through images, light, and shadow. If nothing else, she could come away from this time in South Haven with a new understanding of herself. And that was worth something.

The air was fresh with spring breezes and it seemed like most of South Haven was out enjoying the day. Feeling adrift, Laura tried to lose herself in taking pictures.

She found plenty of subjects on the pier. There was a man and woman chatting as the woman carried a guitar case. Laura adjusted her exposure to properly capture the dark skin tone of a little girl in braids and barrettes. She made more adjustments when she took a photo of a fair-skinned girl.

Some of Laura's bleak mood lifted a little as she shot. It felt good to do something instead of moping, and she felt more confident now taking portraits. She peered through the lens as she scanned the pier for more subjects.

Her chest seized when she caught the profile of a blond man in glasses. Was it…? Maybe Spencer hadn't left!

She took a hesitant step toward him, a smile starting to bloom. Then her heart sank when the man turned around and it wasn't Spencer, after all. Just a random guy who looked a little like him.

"Come on, Frank," she said to her dog. "Let's go."

As she and Frank walked slowly to the gallery, Laura called Rose. "Hey, it's me."

"What's up?" her friend asked. "You sound upset."

Gosh, she must really sound like a downer. "Do you have Tyler's number?"

"But…what about Spencer?"

Laura squeezed her eyes shut for a moment. Clearly, her feelings for Spencer had been evident to everyone.

"His girlfriend showed up this morning," she said. "Then they went home."

"Oh, Laura." Rose's voice was heavy with sympathy. "Maybe you want to wait before calling Tyler."

"No, I'm going to text him today." The sooner she got herself back in the dating world, maybe the sooner the pain of her Spencer-induced heartbreak would fade.

"If you're sure, I can get it from Kenny. Do you want me to come over? We could commiserate over a pint of ice cream."

Rose's concern and willingness to help touched Laura. No wonder they had been best friends since freshman orientation.

"Maybe later. I'm going in to the gallery."

"Okay," her friend said with obvious reluctance. "But if you change your mind, I'm just a text or call away."

"Thank you, Rose," Laura said. "Can you text me Tyler's number when you get it from Kenny?"

"Sure thing. Oh, hey, I think the baby moved! He wants to kick Spencer's butt because he hurt you."

Laura struggled to keep from sniffling. "You're the best."

"I know. That's why you didn't murder me when I ruined your yellow dress."

"Bye, Rose." Laura smiled as she ended the call.

She looked down at Frank and spoke to her pet. "I'm going to be fine. I'll get on with my life and forget I ever knew Spencer Hodkins."

Her dog gave her a dubious look, and she realized neither of them believed her.

Sitting at the bar, Laura swirled wine around her glass and wondered how long she had to sit here, listening to Tyler chatter on about snowboarding, before she could claim that she was tired and go home.

This date was a definite failure. Sure, Tyler was cute, and maybe there had been a time in her life that she might have gone out with someone like him, but that time was over.

"So, anyway," Tyler said animatedly, "we finish the run and got back to the chalet, when we realized we'd left Bobby up on the hill. Oh, that guy," he continued, chuckling, "I'll tell you." He took a drink of his beer.

*What was I thinking?* "Tyler, can I ask you something?"

"Yeah, shoot," he said.

She couldn't believe she was asking this question, but she had to know. "Where do you see yourself in five years?"

He looked at her with disbelief as he plucked a

nut from a nearby bowl. "Me? I don't know where I'm going to be in five weeks." With a shrug, he chucked the nut onto the bar. "But," he added with a grin, "I know in five minutes I'll buy you another drink." He lifted his beer and clinked it against her wineglass. "And cheers!"

Laura sipped her wine and then decided she'd put them both out of their misery. "You know what? I had a long day and I'm wiped out. I think I'd better head home." She stood and picked up her purse.

"Aw, that's too bad." He brightened. "Maybe we could do this again sometime?"

"Maybe," she said, but her tone made it clear that what she really said was *Don't bet on it.* "I'm going to call myself a ride."

"I could see you home," he offered, but then his gaze drifted to the television above the bar. A basketball game had snared his attention.

"That's okay," she said, but she didn't need to bother. She'd already lost him to the playoffs.

Outside, she used the app on her phone to snare a lift. The night was cold and she let it revive her from the incredibly boring conversation she'd just sat through. When the car arrived, she climbed in and gave the driver directions back to the house. The driver took off and mercifully didn't seem to want to chat. Laura spent the ride looking out the window, remembering how excited she had been driving from the train station on her first day in South Haven. Little had she known what had awaited her.

She didn't regret coming here. Not at all. But she still hurt.

After letting herself in at the too-empty rental house, she walked straight to the record player and put on the album she and Spencer had danced to. When the lovely romantic tune began to play, she drifted outside to light the fire pit. Sitting down, she warmed herself by the blaze. She smiled when Frank climbed into her lap.

"You're a good boy," she said softly to her pet. "I'm sorry you miss your cat friend."

Frank looked at her with patient, soulful eyes, and she realized that one of the reasons why she loved dogs so much was that they asked for so little but gave everything.

She nuzzled the top of his head before tilting her head back to look at the night sky. The eternal stars eased her pain a bit as they reminded her that all things in the universe eventually changed and passed by. The heartbreak she felt would someday end—though right now, it seemed like it would never stop.

Wherever he was, she hoped Spencer was moving on, and that he'd find happiness.

# Chapter Eighteen

Since he had gotten back to Chicago a couple of days ago, Spencer felt himself sleepwalking through life. His apartment seemed like someone else's place, save for Mozart asleep on his bed and photos of his parents displayed on bookshelves. When he looked out his windows, he kept hoping for views of the lake, but all he saw was the windows of the apartments across the way.

He and Susan hadn't spoken much, either. She didn't come over and had been slow to return his texts and phone calls. It was probably for the best right now, since he could barely concentrate on eating at regular times let alone have a meaningful conversation with anyone.

Today was the day of his dissertation defense. He

needed to snap out of whatever funk or mood clouded him, and he had to do it quickly.

He'd dropped off copies of his paper with his dissertation committee, and due to timing with the academic year and Dr. Drake's need to move the grant money process along, they'd fast-tracked his defense to noon today.

As he sat with his smoothie, Susan texted him: *Good luck. I'll see you on campus?*

It wasn't gushing with warmth and affection, but she wasn't giving him the silent treatment, either.

*Can't keep me away*, he answered, but the truth was that he was having a hard time remembering why any of this was so important.

He debated whether or not to text Laura—not only was today the defense of his dissertation, but it was also the big art fair in South Haven. The gallery hosted a sizeable reception, including revealing who the artist would be for the New Artists Gallery. Laura had been working very hard on making sure everything came together, and he wanted to wish her luck.

Not only was he not supposed to contact Laura, he didn't even have her phone number. The thought made him laugh humorlessly. It felt like everything was falling apart. He should be excited, or at least nervous about the upcoming defense, and all he could feel was…nothing. Numbness.

Without Laura's smile greeting him every morning, he didn't know why he needed to get out of bed. If she wasn't there to encourage him as he worked, what was the point?

He sighed heavily before finishing his smoothie and placing his dirty glass in the crowded sink. Normally, he washed his dishes immediately after using them, but even something that he enjoyed—like dishes—barely registered. Anyway, he needed to get ready for the defense.

Slipping his arms into his navy blazer, he checked his reflection in the hallway mirror. A man with dull, listless eyes stared back at him. He tried to smile at himself, but it felt too strained and he gave up.

When Mozart twined between his legs, he reached down to pet her. "Wishing me luck, too?"

She butted her head against his hand, but there was something a bit lethargic in it. He would have thought that she was sick the way she'd been avoiding her food, yet he knew his cat and her moods. "Sorry, Moz. I know you miss Frank. I also miss...him."

Mozart watched as Spencer grabbed his briefcase that held a copy of his dissertation. He slung the strap onto his shoulder and the bag seemed weighted with bricks.

"When I get back," he said to the cat, "you'll get a celebratory can of tuna."

She didn't even blink as she ambled back into the bedroom for her midmorning nap. Spencer wished he could join her.

The ride on the train sped past in a blur. His movements were mechanical as he got off at the stop for the campus, and as he walked to the psychology department. It wasn't usual for PhDs to finish their program as quickly as Spencer had, or as young, but he'd been extremely dedicated and had taken on a double course load to ensure he got his doctorate before he was twenty-five. Now he wondered what the rush had been.

At the psychology department, Diego, the administrator, pointed him to an auditorium—which seated two hundred people.

"I thought we were just going to meet in a classroom," Spencer said in surprise.

"Normally we do, but Dr. Drake wanted it in the auditorium. Something about setting up a video camera at the back." Diego lifted his eyebrows. "I guess he wants to record it."

Spencer knew why. If Dr. Drake liked Spencer's dissertation and defense, he would take the video to potential investors for further research.

*Great. Just what I need—more pressure.*

"Want some coffee? Wine?" Diego teased.

Spencer smiled politely. "I think I'm good. Going to head over now."

Diego picked up the phone. "I'll let them know you're coming."

The hallways were empty since most students were still on spring break. His steps echoed loudly as he walked to the auditorium. He sat on a bench outside the assigned room, and as he waited, his mind drifted.

How was the art fair going? He wished he could be there to see it—and Laura. Had she missed him these past few days the way he'd missed her? Hopefully, she'd gotten on with her life and had filed him away in her personal history. But he knew that no matter what the future held for him, he would never forget her. He doubted that he'd ever be able to sing "Fly Me to the Moon" again without thinking of her in that black wig and sequined miniskirt.

"Spencer?"

He blinked and saw Susan standing in front of him.

"They're ready for you," she said briskly.

He stood and tugged on his jacket. She stepped closer and brushed her hands over his lapels, removing any tiny bits of lint or dust. Her movements were fast and businesslike, as was her tone when she asked, "Where were you?"

"Nowhere," he said. "Right here."

She nodded, and moved away from him to open

the door to the lecture hall. At her look, he followed her inside.

"On the stage," Susan said, pointing him toward it. On the stage, a lectern bearing the university's insignia awaited him. Feeling like a man walking up the steps to the chopping block, Spencer climbed the stairs to the stage. He squinted under the bright lights but could just make out the members of his committee sitting in the third row. A little farther away sat Susan with her father. Spencer couldn't see Dr. Drake's expression, but if Susan had told her father anything about Spencer's lies, surely her dad was ready to throttle him.

Presumably, somewhere in the darkness was a camera, recording Spencer. So if Dr. Drake *was* angry with him, he kept his eyes on the funding prize.

Spencer swallowed hard. This was it. The end of years of hard work and two weeks of frantic writing. Two weeks that had changed him completely.

"Good afternoon," he said into the microphone, "professors, faculty members, and distinguished guests." He paused to look down at his dissertation. "*The Chemistry of Love: A Study in Psychobiology and Human Emotion*, by Spencer Hodkins."

He cleared his throat and looked out into the vast darkness of the auditorium, feeling utterly lost.

Despite Laura's low mood over the past few days, she felt jumpy with excitement as people lined up outside for the big opening. She'd dressed carefully today, wearing a cute flowered dress she had bought at a local boutique, and made certain her hair and makeup were nice so that she would be a good representative of Ellen and the gallery.

All morning, she and the older woman had been preparing the gallery for the reception. Nearly everything was done—the canapés were displayed and there was plenty of wine, champagne, and sodas.

Plastic champagne glasses stood waiting on the counter of the reception desk. Thinking that they'd need more, Laura rummaged beneath the desk.

A large open box full of paper snagged her attention, and when she caught sight of her own face on a picture clipped to one of the sheets, she hefted the box onto the desk.

Her picture was attached to the same questionnaire that she'd filled out for the rental company, and both of those were clipped to a photo of Spencer and *his* questionnaire.

*What on earth can this mean?*

She dug through the box and found more pictures and more questionnaires, all of them paired up. People of all genders had been matched together. Laura saw that the paired-up questionnaires had similar answers—the way she and Spencer had written the same answers.

"We're getting quite a crowd out there." Ellen walked up, oblivious to Laura's discovery. "Maybe I'd better open the doors early."

Laura held up her and Spencer's questionnaires and photographs. "Ellen, what is this?"

The older woman looked briefly surprised before she gave Laura a smile. But she didn't look apologetic or embarrassed. "I forgot that was in there."

"It's my application form and Spencer's application form—clipped together. And there are a ton of other ones too, all clipped together as well. In pairs." She stared at the woman she had come to consider a friend. "What have you been up to?"

Ellen took one of the open champagne bottles and poured two glasses. "My husband and I loved that house. And after he passed away, I couldn't bear to live in it alone. But I had promised him that it would always be filled with love."

Comprehension dawned on Laura, and a slow smile spread across her face. She ought to have known. It had been in front of her the whole time. Instead of feeling angry, though, she was filled with admiration and appreciation. What a sly lady Ellen was!

"You do this on purpose," Laura said. "Double-book the house to bring people together. That's why the questionnaires were so personal. You're matchmaking." She brought people together, giving them the gift of love. What an amazing thing to do.

Ellen made a sound of agreement as she handed Laura champagne. "It's a little bit sneaky, perhaps, but so far it's always worked out."

Heaviness settled in Laura's chest as she thought of herself and Spencer. "Until now."

"Spring isn't over yet, dear." With a mysterious smile, Ellen clinked her glass against Laura's. After she took a sip, she said cheerfully, "Speaking of spring, it's time to open the gallery. Shall we?"

Laura set her glass down and went to the gallery door. At Ellen's nod, she opened it and said to the crowd, "We are open!"

People filed in, all of them eager to see what the Davis Gallery had for their art viewing pleasure. Several guests grabbed champagne on their way in before dispersing into the different display spaces. A few looked with interest at the curtain hiding the entrance to the New Artists Gallery.

Two men in stylish clothes approached Laura as she stood off to one side. "Who's the New Artist this year?" one of them asked.

She spread her hands. "I don't know! My boss won't tell me. Said it was supposed to be a surprise for everyone."

"Aren't you dying of curiosity?" the other man asked.

"I am, but those are the rules." She smiled wistfully to herself, thinking of Spencer and how he'd had so many rules when they first met.

What was he doing now? Doctoral candidates defended their theses, so maybe Spencer was in the middle of that. She hoped he was killing it.

The couple moved away, and Ellen brought over another pair of guests. "Would you take these ladies on a tour of the main gallery? They'd love to hear from someone with a trained eye."

Laura briefly stared at that description of herself. Then she realized that her eye *had* become trained, and she felt a surge of confidence.

She led the guests through the gallery, talking at length about the composition and subject matter of each photo. It seemed like she made sense, too, because the women nodded and looked thoughtful at each comment.

Laura stopped in front of a large black-and-white print. "The artist is making a statement not only in his use of light and shadow, but also in the depth of focus he's chosen."

"Good point! Thank you so much for your time," one of the guests said. "I think all this art calls for some refreshment."

"Of course." Laura waved them toward the table with drinks and hors d'oeuvres.

As the women walked away, Ellen appeared. "I'd say this is quite the success," the older woman said. "Wouldn't you?"

"Definitely. But what about the annex?" Laura asked. "People have been asking me who it is this year."

"I guess it's time," Ellen said. "Would you give me a hand?"

Laura walked with Ellen to the curtained entrance to the New Artists Gallery and waited as the gallery owner spoke.

"Hello? Everyone, could I have your attention please?" When the crowd gathered and quieted down, Ellen continued. "Good afternoon and welcome to the South Haven Art Fair here at the Davis Gallery."

Ellen's gaze moved across the guests as she continued. "Every year, I have chosen a new photographer to feature here at the gallery, someone with a fresh vision and an original eye all their own. And sometimes it takes an out-of-towner to see our little village in a new way, and that's certainly the case this year." She paused and smiled. "It gives me great pleasure to present the Davis Gallery Emerging Artist for this year."

Ellen motioned to Laura, and they both pulled back the heavy velvet curtains. Laura peered eagerly into the annex.

Her mouth fell open as she saw her photographs on the walls, as well as a placard with her picture, name, and biography printed on it.

"Laura Haley," Ellen announced as the guests clapped.

Too stunned to move, Laura let the crowd move around her on their way into the gallery showing *her photographs*. She turned and looked with shock at Ellen.

"Surprised?" Ellen asked.

"I can't believe it!" Laura nodded as a guest offered her congratulations. "Thank you." She and Ellen moved into the annex, and everywhere Laura looked were the pictures she'd taken during her two weeks in South Haven. Patrons and art lovers stood in front of the images, nodding in appreciation. "These are my photographs. In a gallery. And people really like them."

"Of course they do, dear," Ellen answered. "They're good."

Laura could hardly comprehend that her work was deemed worthy enough to be in a gallery—and yet here it was, on display for everyone to see.

"I don't know how I can ever thank you," she said.

"Would you consider staying on with me?" Ellen asked. "I could certainly use someone of your talent here."

Laura blinked at her. "You mean, stay in South Haven?"

"I'm thinking of starting a school of my own, just small at first. A few classes, but you never know where these things might lead."

The world rushed around Laura at a hundred miles an hour. What Ellen suggested was a complete upheaval. "I don't know," she said slowly.

"I realize that it is quite a big commitment but… you just think it over, okay?" Ellen gave her arm a squeeze before leaving Laura alone to contemplate the chance of a whole new life.

As she considered this, her gaze fell on her portrait of Spencer. Ellen had included it in the exhibition. Seeing his handsome face again made all the unhappiness she'd felt over the past few days come rushing back. That sadness crashed right into her excitement over the possibility of changing everything in her world, making Laura dizzy with confusion.

If only she could get in touch with Spencer to tell him about Ellen's offer.

If only she could think of life without him.

# Chapter Nineteen

Still riding high on seeing her work displayed in a professional gallery, Laura drifted around the art show in a golden glow. When she spotted Kenny and Rose at the refreshments table, she rushed immediately over.

"You made it!" she said as she approached her friends.

"We're so proud of you," Kenny said, hugging her. Rose also gave her a tight squeeze.

"Thank you." Laura shook her head. "It's kind of overwhelming."

"So," Rose said, "what now?"

"Now..." Laura realized then exactly what she had to do. Hopefully, she'd have the courage to actually do it. "I'm going to tell my parents that I finally know what I want to do with my life. And then I'm going to tell them I love them. And then…" She took a deep breath. "I'm going to say, 'I quit.'"

Rose and Kenny exchanged looks of surprise. "You're really going to do that?" he asked.

"Yeah." It was going to be terrifying, but she needed to take this next step and grow up at last. She'd discovered so much about herself these past two weeks, and while the lessons had sometimes been painful, she was glad she'd learned them. "They're going to be angry, and there's going to be some yelling, but it's what I want to do."

"Get ready." Rose looked over Laura's shoulder. "Here comes your chance."

Laura turned and stared in astonishment as her parents walked by, examining the artwork. Her father wore his usual "going out" blazer and her mother sported her favorite special occasion earrings. Momentarily forgetting Rose and Kenny, Laura strode up to her parents.

"Mom? Dad?" Both her parents greeted her with smiles as she approached. "Hi! What are you guys doing here?"

After they hugged, her mother said, "We had a phone call from a lady who said you were showing some of your photographs in her gallery."

"You didn't think we'd miss our daughter's first big

show, do you?" Her father chuckled at the absurdity of the thought.

"Let's go take a look, Ed," her mother said, hooking her arm through her husband's and pulling him into the New Artists Gallery.

Laura trailed after them as they looked at her work. Her stomach was a mass of fluttering while she studied their faces. Both of them weren't particularly effusive people, so it was hard to read their expressions. Finally, she couldn't take it any longer.

"So," she asked nervously, "what do you think?"

Her mother's eyes shone with happy tears. "It's beautiful, sweetie."

"Very impressed, honey," her father said. "I mean, you've always had a camera in your hand, but who knew?"

"Thank you. Both of you." Laura's heart took flight, thrilled with her parents' praise. She should have known that they would support her, whatever she chose to do. They had always been there for her, even when she'd been spinning in confused circles.

But maybe they might not support her in every endeavor. Gathering her nerve, she said, "Mom, Dad, I have to tell you something."

Her parents suddenly looked nervous. Her dad shifted on his feet, and her mother twisted her hands together the way she always did when she was anxious about something. Laura tensed.

"Actually," her mom said hesitantly, "we have something we need to tell you first." She nudged her husband. "Ed?"

Her father let out a long exhalation. "Your mother and I..." He jingled the keys in his pocket. "We sold the business."

"What?" Laura couldn't possibly be hearing right. Her whole life, Haley & Haley had been the backbone of her parents' relationship. They talked, ate, and slept accounting. But now they'd gone and sold the bedrock of their existence?

"We're going to take some time off and travel," her mom explained. "See the world for a bit."

As Laura continued to gape, her dad said in a calming voice, "We put a little money away for you, but I'm afraid from now on, honey, you're on your own."

"Wow." Laura couldn't possibly say more than that one syllable. It was like someone discovering that you could get electricity from cupcakes.

"What did you want to tell us?" her mom asked.

Laura held up a hand. "Wait a minute. It's April. You can't just sell the business in the middle of tax season."

"Technically," her father said, "Haley & Haley will

no longer be ours as of May first. We asked for time to get our clients' filings in, of course."

"How long have you been planning this?" Laura asked.

Her parents shared a sheepish look. "Since last November," her mom said. "We didn't say anything because we weren't sure if the sale was going to go through. It didn't seem fair to worry you unnecessarily. But the transaction became final yesterday, and now you know."

Laura put a hand to her forehead as she absorbed this information. Her steady, unchanging parents were taking a huge step. Everything in their lives was about to change.

If they could do it, so could she. "I think I can tell you my news, too."

It was early evening by the time Laura made it back to the rental house. She'd left her stunned but pleased parents at the gallery, with promises that they'd get breakfast tomorrow before they headed back to Lansing. There were a lot of plans to make, but she and her folks had been eager to start the next chapters in their lives.

Laura stepped inside the foyer of the house, calling

for her dog. "Frank! Guess what? I'm a photographer. A real live photographer." She headed into the kitchen. "Come on. Let's go for a walk and celebrate."

Her words faltered when she spotted a bottle of white wine chilling on the kitchen counter with two glasses beside it. She most definitely hadn't put any of that out before leaving this morning. Unless that meant…? *Not more matchmaking. The last attempt nearly killed me.* Her heart still ached from losing Spencer before they'd even had a chance to find out what they'd be like together.

"Hello?" she called. "Is somebody here? I'm renting this house."

The door to the back patio opened. She gasped when Spencer strode inside, beaming at her.

"There must have been some sort of mix-up," he said sunnily.

Her heart seemed to leap up into the sky as a stunned laugh broke from her. "What are you doing here? I thought you had to present your paper."

"I did." He pulled the cork from the bottle and poured them each some wine. "And it did *not* go very well."

Her elation flattened at this news. "What? What happened?"

"They said they felt I didn't believe what I was

saying. If I wasn't buying it, why should they?" He didn't seem especially disappointed, though.

"So what are you going to do?" He'd been all about his plans. Surely he would be in a panic by now if those plans had fallen apart. Yet, if anything, he seemed lighter. Happier.

"Start over." He looked at her warmly, his eyes a brilliant blue that seemed to overflow with tenderness. "You know of a place I could stay for a while to work on it?"

Despite the joy lifting inside of her, she asked, "What about Susan?" Her resolve not to break them up held firm.

"Susan." His lips curved. "I tried to make s'mores for her in the apartment and I set fire to the drapes, so..." He shrugged.

"You're kidding," she said in disbelief.

"Actually," he said with a tip of his head, "I am. The truth is," he continued, looking at her with so much adoration she lost her breath, "I'm in love with you. And there is no place else that I would rather be."

She thought she could fly up to the roof and beyond, all the way up to the stars. The love she felt for him threatened to spill out of her like an overflowing cup. Words formed on her lips, and yet she knew they weren't the right words. They'd begun their life together two weeks ago when Mozart and Frank—and their owners—had started fighting.

"We're probably going to have to make up a few more rules," she said playfully, "if we're going to be under the same roof." Her emotions were too strong to approach them head-on.

Spencer looked very pleased by the idea that they'd be living together. He closed the distance between them. "Let's start with rule number one." He bent to kiss her and she lifted onto her toes to meet him halfway, eagerly anticipating the feel of his lips on hers.

"Hello?" Ellen's voice rang out from the entryway. "Excuse me?"

Laura and Spencer broke apart in time to see Ellen come forward, holding Laura's camera.

"You forgot your camera in the gallery, dear," Ellen said with gentle remonstrance. "You really need to be a little more careful."

"Thank you." Laura's cheeks felt hot and she knew that she looked like a woman about to receive a passionate kiss.

"Spencer," Ellen said as she turned to him. "I wondered when you'd be back."

He frowned in confusion. "How did you—"

Oh, boy, was there a lot of explaining to do. Before Laura could say anything, Ellen glanced outside and exclaimed, "The light is absolutely perfect right now. Come on." She waved Spencer and Laura toward the patio doors. "Outside. Let's go. This is going to be a great picture."

As Laura and Spencer headed to the patio, she glanced back to see Frank and Mozart happily curled up on the sofa together. She smiled to see the two pets snuggling so closely.

*They knew*, she thought as Ellen snapped a picture of Laura and Spencer embracing. *Frank and Mozart both knew all along.*

# Epilogue

*Six months later*

Laura smoothed a shaky hand down the front of her beaded lace dress as she heard the musicians start to play the processional. It wasn't the traditional bridal march. Instead, she and Spencer had picked "Spring" from Vivaldi's *Four Seasons.*

Wearing a smart russet-colored suit, her mother appeared behind her and squeezed her shoulders.

"They're waiting for you," her mother said excitedly. "Are you ready?"

"I think so." Laura turned to face her mother, her hands slippery on her bouquet of autumnal roses and anemones. "Promise me if I start to faint that you'll cause a distraction."

"I'm ready to shoot the fireworks," her dad said. Both he and her mom were deeply tanned from their nonstop traveling—but they had come home for the occasion of their only daughter's wedding. Two days ago, they'd flown in from Morocco, and her mother's suit was accented with a beautiful Moroccan scarf.

Her mother patted her face. "It won't be necessary because you're going to be fine. Spencer, on the other hand, might need medical assistance. He was breathing into a paper bag ten minutes ago."

Laura gave a horrified laugh. "Poor guy! Let's end his suffering." She took her dad's offered elbow and together they left the reception room of the botanical garden. They had opted for this venue here in South Haven because it had become one of Laura and Spencer's favorites.

As Laura and her family walked toward the rose garden where the ceremony was going to take place, she inhaled deeply, steadying herself. These past six months had been full of upheaval, most of it good. She and Spencer had rented lakeside cottages, and he'd written his new dissertation there: "The Chemistry of Love: How Love Changes Our Neurochemistry for the Better."

Soon after he'd defended his dissertation, Dr. Philip Drake had given Spencer a grant so he could further his research in the subject. That had been a surprise, given who Dr. Drake was, but the professor knew important research when he saw it. A university close to South Haven had been more than happy to host Spencer as he started work on a more expansive project that he hoped to turn into a book.

In the meantime, Laura and Ellen had been laboring on a photography school. There had been a few setbacks, mostly involving logistics, but the school was set to open next spring, offering classes for children and retirees, among others. Laura could hardly wait to start teaching. Her own photography had progressed significantly from the spring show, and a gallery in Detroit wanted to have her in a solo exhibition next year.

Dating Spencer had been the happiest experience of Laura's existence. There had definitely been adjustments, yet those wrinkles only added spice and color to their lives.

It had been made even better when, as they'd camped on the Upper Peninsula, he'd accepted her marriage proposal. Today, they'd join their lives together forever.

She and her parents now paused at the top of the aisle. Friends and family turned to look at her make her entrance, but all she saw was Spencer, devastatingly handsome in his tuxedo, and looking just a little pale. His pallor faded when he caught sight of her, and a huge smile wreathed his face. Standing beside him as best man, Spencer's grandfather beamed and patted Spencer on his shoulder.

Ellen led Frank on a leash down the aisle. Her dog wore a flower on his collar and carried a basket full of petals, and as Ellen and Frank walked, she took petals from the basket and scattered them on the floor. The crowd chuckled to see the dog acting as flower girl—but there was no way he could be left out of today.

Slowly, on her father's arm, Laura made her way toward her future husband, the lilting strains of Vivaldi floating on the air. Her heart pounded with each step. As she took her place on one side of the officiant, she winked at matron of honor Rose, who held Mozart. The wedding rings were threaded on Mozart's collar. The cat was definitely getting a can of tuna for being so patient today.

Her father gave Laura a final kiss before taking his seat beside her mother in the front row. Both her mom and Spencer's grandmother dabbed at their eyes.

"Dearly beloved..."

Laura and Spencer smiled shyly at each other. Six and a half months ago, neither of them had known what lay in store for them. What had at first been an annoyance and inconvenience had turned into the greatest gift either of them had ever known.

# S'mores French Toast

*A Hallmark Original Recipe*

When Laura goes grocery shopping with health-food-obsessed Spencer, she can hardly believe that he's never had s'mores. Later, when she persuades him to try one, he has to admit it's pretty good. So is this recipe for *S'mores French Toast,* made with buttery-crisp griddled brioche, toasted marshmallows, melty dark chocolate, and graham cracker crumbs, served with fresh berries.

**Yield:** 2 sandwiches (4 servings)
**Prep Time:** 20 minutes
**Cook Time:** 20 minutes

## INGREDIENTS

Graham Cracker Crumble:

- ¾ cup graham cracker crumbs
- 3 tablespoons melted butter
- 1 tablespoon sugar

Chocolate Ganache:

- 1 cup heavy cream
- 1 cup semi-sweet chocolate chips

French Toast:

- 2 eggs, lightly beaten
- ¾ cup half and half
- ½ teaspoon vanilla extract
- 2 tablespoons butter
- 4 slices country bread, ½-inch thick

- 12 large marshmallows
- As needed, blueberries
- As needed, maple syrup

## DIRECTIONS

1. Preheat oven to 350°F.

2. To prepare graham cracker crumble: combine graham cracker crumbs, melted butter and sugar in a bowl and mix to blend. Press the crumb mixture into the bottom of a small pie

pan. Bake for 4 to 5 minutes, or until lightly browned. Cool; crumble into pieces.

3. To prepare chocolate ganache: Bring heavy cream to a simmer, stirring occasionally; pour over chocolate chips and let stand for 10 minutes. Whisk until smooth and creamy. If making ahead, chocolate ganache can be reheated in microwave in 10 second increments until melted, stirring frequently.

4. To prepare French toast: combine eggs, half and half, and vanilla in a shallow bowl and whisk to blend. Melt butter in a large heavy skillet over medium heat. Dip bread slices in egg mixture; drain excess and griddle on each side for 3 minutes, or until golden.

5. Preheat broiler. Place marshmallows on baking sheet; run under broiler until puffy and lightly toasted.

6. To assemble each s'mores French toast sandwich: arrange 6 toasted marshmallows on 1 slice of warm French toast; drizzle warm chocolate ganache over marshmallows. Top with 1 slice of French toast, forming a sandwich. Top, as needed, with a drizzle of chocolate ganache, blueberries, maple syrup

and graham cracker crumbles. Cut sandwich in half. Repeat with remaining s'mores French toast components to make additional sandwiches.

Thanks so much for reading *Like Cats and Dogs*. We hope you enjoyed it!

You might also like these other ebooks from Hallmark Publishing:

*Journey Back to Christmas*
*Christmas in Homestead*
*Love You Like Christmas*
*A Heavenly Christmas*
*A Dash of Love*
*Moonlight in Vermont*

For information about our new releases and exclusive offers, sign up for our free newsletter!

You can also connect with us here:

Facebook.com/HallmarkPublishing

Twitter.com/HallmarkPublish